# GREGG STEWART

KIM REAPER © 2025 Gregg Stewart

Published by Graveside Press 2025
graveside-press.com



Editing: Poppy McDonald and Kelley York
Cover illustration: Sleepy Fox Studio
Interior Formatting: Sleepy Fox Studio
Digital 978-1-967547-59-3
Paperback (KDP) 978-1-967547-56-2
Paperback (Trade) 978-1-967547-57-9
Hardcover 978-1-967547-58-6

# Content Notes

*Although Kim Reaper deals with the heaviness of loss and mental health, it's also a beautiful look into why life (and death) are important, familial love, and how different people process their grief—and how they hide it.*

*For a list of potentially triggering content, please visit our website, or skip to page 178.*

*Many children believe
a monster is hiding in their closet,
but the smart ones know
the only safe hiding place is the closet
because monsters are everywhere.*

# One

Kim's bedroom is a celebration of her former self, an homage to all things happy, and of those simpler times when her parents were still alive. A carousel horse mobile, handmade by her mother, hangs from the ceiling, suspended by fuzzy periwinkle streamers. Glow-in-the-dark moons and stars pepper the ceiling. Six unicorn figurines rest on the pink dresser. A silver-framed photo of a majorette sits on the nightstand, her face aglow as she leads the band down Main Street.

Kim's bedroom shimmers with pre-teen nostalgia, and yet, the effects of time march ever onward. One of the unicorn figurines has a cracked horn. Another has a missing tail. A thin layer of dust covers the mobile. A few moons and stars have fallen from the ceiling, leaving behind pale glue outlines. Rainbow cupcake stickers, peeling at their edges, freckle the faded blue and pink striped walls. The worn strawberry patchwork quilt that frequents the four-poster bed is missing. So is Kim.

She sits in the dark, running the movie behind closed eyes—a slide show of every memory she's retained of her parents. At age three, on a swing set, her mother smiling, pushing her, both laughing. Christmas morning, age six, her father opening the ceramic coffee mug she made for him emblazoned with "Best Daddy Ever" in blue ink, his favorite color. Kim recalls his smile, the joy and pride. Switching fast, because the memories are now jumbled together like a fast edit of old film reels played and replayed until the reel begins to degrade from wear. Kim's last summer road trip with them, singing songs together at the top of their lungs. Kim has run through this reel of memories ten-thousand times since they died, hoping to hold on to their laughter, the look and sound of it, but it's all fading. She squeezes her eyes tighter, bending her will to try to keep them alive, at least in her mind.

Jake saunters into Kim's bedroom without knocking and peers around in search of his sister. Today is the first day of his last year of high school, so it's important—no, *imperative*—Kim and her awkwardness do not trash his hard-won reputation as the coolest guy at Sutherland High.

"Kimmy?"

Kim can tell from her older brother's tone he's already annoyed she's not downstairs at breakfast. She knows she can't hide in here all day. *The longer he looks, the madder he'll get.*

Her small voice calls from the closet. "Yeah?"

Heavy footsteps stride to the closet door. It swings open, revealing a fifteen-year-old girl wrapped in a strawberry patchwork quilt. Jake's expression does little to hide his distain. "What the... Did you sleep in here?"

Kim stares up at her older brother—the golden boy everyone adores. Their praises echo through her mind: *"Oh Jake, you're so good at baseball. Oh Jake, you're so intelligent and handsome. And those cheekbones!"* Kim wants to puke.

*"Never better"* is Jake's reply anytime someone asks him how he's doing. Kim cannot comprehend how Jake's been able to accept the way things are when they've been unacceptable for over four years—and will never be acceptable again. *How does he stay so optimistic when Mom and Dad are...dead?*

"Seriously, Kimmy, did you sleep in your closet?" Jake's tone scares Kim sometimes. It's like he only gets mad when it comes to her.

Kim pulls the strawberry blanket tighter around her and looks up at him with puppy-dog eyes. "I heard a noise last night."

Jake bites his lower lip as he regards his kid sister. "A noise? Like what?"

Kim edges deeper into the closet amongst a small mountain of musty stuffed animals and mismatched shoes. "Something scraping outside my door."

"Oh, you mean the crazed serial-killer dragging his axe down the hall. That noise?"

Kim's eyes fill with terror.

Jake laughs. "That was just Grandma shuffling her nasty, worn-out slippers to the bathroom, you weirdo. Come on out, we're already late."

"Do I have to go?"

"Yes! You do, Kimmy. Only losers ditch their first day of high school. And marching band tryouts are this afternoon, remember?"

Kim gasps and lurches, sending stuffed animals in all directions. *Tryouts!* She jumps from the closet to gather her clothes.

Jake blocks the door. "Wait. What are you wearing?"

Kim holds up a crumpled bundle of pink overalls, a white t-shirt emblazoned with *Keep Calm & Bake Cupcakes* in rainbow font, and her hand-painted blue mermaid high-top sneakers.

Jake recoils as if her outfit was a garland of garlic to his vampiric sense of style. "You gotta be kidding me."

"What's wrong with it?"

Jake looks away and groans as he surveys the bedroom. "I mean, when are you gonna redecorate in here and get some new clothes? Don't ya think you're a little old for this look?"

Kim scowls, narrowing her eyes at her brother. "Um, Dad painted these striped walls, and Mom got me those cupcake stickers, and this t-shirt, and that carousel mobile, and my quilt that smells like strawberries, so yeah, like, no Jake, I'm not changing any of it."

Jake exhales, exasperated. He's always *sooo exasperated* with her. "They were my parents too, y'know? I miss 'em all the time, but Kimmy, it's been almost five years."

"Four years, seven months, and twenty-one days."

Jake's lips press together and go white as he bites back an outburst. "Wow. Yep, four years, seven months, and twenty-one days. You gotta move on, Kimmy. You're fifteen, not ten. You're starting high school today. Time to grow up."

Kim glares daggers at Jake. He's right of course, but she's miffed he had the nerve to say it.

The tension of the moment breaks with a gravel-throated call from downstairs. "You kids eatin' breakfast or what?"

Jake cocks his head to yell out the door. "Be right there, Grandma!" He turns to his sister. "Fine. Wear what you want."

"Fine, I will." Kim looks down at the clothes in her arms, and now she isn't so sure. Tears well in her eyes, and it makes her even madder.

Kim's distress doesn't go unnoticed and Jake's tone softens. "Really, wear whatever. It's cool. You should feel comfortable on your first day. Forget I said anything. Don't be upset. It'll stress out Grandma." He leans forward, getting to Kim's eye level. "Hey, take a deep breath. Go wash your face. Brush your teeth. And come to breakfast. It's all good."

"I just wish Mom and Dad—"

"Hey, stop. Just stop." Jake grows impatient, but then he sucks in his breath and tries to calm Kim like their mother always knew how. "You can do this, you got this, okay?"

"What if something happens to her?"

"What? To who?"

"Grandma. What if—"

"Listen, hey, nothing's gonna happen to Grandma."

Kim wants to believe her brother, but she's heading down a spiral now, thinking about all the ways she might lose someone else she loves. She's stuck, refusing to grow up, and doesn't know how to get herself unstuck.

Jake's brief dance with empathy comes to an abrupt halt, like when the song stops during a game of musical chairs. He backs away. "Christ, Kimmy, why you gotta be so *life-a-phobic*?"

His words snatch Kim's tears back before they can fall.

Jake storms out the door. "If you're not downstairs in ten minutes, I'm leaving without you. Take the bus. Whatever."

Kim squeezes her clothes to her chest and counts to ten like her father taught her. "I'm not life-a-phobic." *What even is that word? Did he mean panophobic, like, the fear of everything? Stupid. Wrong.*

Kim steps to her doorframe and freezes. Peeking into the hallway, she looks both ways, heart-rate ramping up to hummingbird status. *Thumpthumpthumpthump.* She takes a deep breath before dashing into the bathroom and locking the door behind her. She leans against the door and exhales, having survived the harrowing journey across the hall. *Life-a-phobic? I mean, maybe?*

A lurking black shadow whisks down the hall. A glint of steel catches the morning sunlight. For an instant, it flashes through the narrow space at the top of the doorframe. Kim sees the flash, ducks her face into the sink, and continues brushing her teeth with furious intent.

Ten minutes later, Kim is downstairs at the breakfast table. Grandma is there, wearing her floral housecoat and slippers. Most days, it's all she wears. A cigarette hangs from her lower lip, stuck with the gumminess of day-old apricot lipstick. In front of her is a plate with buttered toast and a mug of coffee, but she doesn't seem interested. She's squeezed fresh orange juice and made an egg scramble for Kim, who stares at the scene, unsure why she's supposed to eat a nutritious breakfast when her grandma subsists on a diet of coffee, toast, and cigarettes. And Jake, *that jerk,* why does he get to look like he's in a boy band with his eight-pack abs and perfect skin? How does he eat sugary cereal and fast-food hamburgers every day and still look like that?

Grandma points her lit cigarette at the empty chair. "Kimmy, c'mon and eat your breakfast." She's got a voice like she's been licking sandpaper every day for a quarter century.

Kim sets down her star unicorn backpack and majorette baton. Jake gets up from the table the moment she sits. As he drops his bowl in the sink for someone else to wash, he points his dirty spoon at Kim's baton. "Oh, so you're not gonna chicken out?"

Kim scoffs through a mouthful of food. "No way."

Grandma exhales smoke all over breakfast as she pats Kim's hand. "I'm sure you'll do great, Kimmy. I bet it's gonna be you leading that band in the Home Day's parade this year, and not that Taylor Mead."

Kim grins, though she wants to groan. *Why did Grandma have to bring up Taylor?* She waves off the comment. "I'm not worried."

Jake cocks his head, makes a face like he's unconvinced. "I dunno, I hear Taylor Mead's pretty good at handling the baton. Throws it real high up there."

Kim gives him some side-eye, and before she can ask, *Yeah, but can she catch it?*, Grandma comes to her defense. "Now Jake, don't be startin' nothin'. You know Kimmy was born to be a majorette—just like her mother. Oh, your mom, she was the prettiest thing that ever led a parade."

Jake grabs his black leather backpack and heads for the door. "Sure, but first she needs to show up at tryouts and quit hiding in her room all day."

Kim extends a hand toward her backpack and baton. "You can clearly see that I'm going."

Jake stands in the open doorway. "Fine, let's go."

Kim crams two more bites of food into her mouth and guzzles her orange juice to wash it down. "That was so yummy, Grandma. You're the absolute best, and I love you *sooo* much."

She jumps into the woman's lap for a big hug. Grandma tosses her cigarette into the ashtray to keep from burning the girl. She pats Kim's back with one hand while pushing her away with the other. "A'right, okay, you have fun today."

Kim heads for the door but pauses when Grandma launches into a coughing fit. Her emphysema is getting worse. Kim doesn't know what to say or do, and she can't understand how Jake doesn't even notice.

Her face pales. "You okay?"

Grandma waves a hand to shoo Kim away as she continues hacking. "Fine, fine, go to school."

Kim sighs as she heads for the car. Jake is already in the driver's seat, laughing and joking with Danny and Brian, who are hitching a ride. The two had been standing in the driveway, taking turns punching one another in the arm while they waited for their hero, Jake, to emerge. They used to come inside, but after they all got caught drinking last year, they're afraid of Grandma.

Jake fires up his father's Mustang as Kim climbs into the backseat. Brian says, "Hey Kimmy," but beyond that, the guys ignore her as they catch up about summer vacations and the upcoming football game against Shadow Valley.

Jakes takes the long way to school to avoid going over the bridge and Kim wonders if he does that for her sake. The boys continue talking, yelling, and ignoring her, so she puts in her earbuds and plays her favorite song on repeat, blocking out their voices. She closes her eyes as the song plays, her memory reel running through her mind on repeat until they arrive at the Sutherland High parking lot.

When Kim exits the vehicle, a sudden sense of dread overtakes her.

*New school. New locker. New teachers. No friends.*

She walks onto campus in lockstep with her brother. Jake does his best to avoid tripping over his kid sister while high-fiving every guy and hugging every girl who looks his way.

*Everybody loves Jake.* Kim looks like his personal assistant standing so close, or maybe the intern to his assistants, Danny and Brian. She doesn't like this lackey reputation she's already cultivating, and the feeling is enough to force her to stray from her brother's orbit and head to the auditorium for first-year orientation. She hears Jake yelling "Never better" in the distance and groans, stepping up her pace.

The moment Kim walks inside the high school auditorium, she knows she's made a huge mistake. Taylor Mead stands at the table, handing out student orientation pamphlets. Kim is sure Taylor's boobs have gone up three sizes since she last saw her. Also, she's dressed like a sorority sister at a frat party in her black tube top, white skirt, and heels. Her hair is perfect. Her teeth are perfect. Her makeup is perfect. Kim can't stand Taylor Mead. From kindergarten to fifth grade, they were inseparable, but now?

Taylor breaks into a wide grin as Kim approaches. "Hey, little baby." It is not a term of endearment.

Taylor's been calling Kim "little baby" for years. She holds out a pamphlet, still smiling. Kim doesn't take it. Taylor waves the paper. "C'mon, little baby, take your first steps." Her friends start to giggle. There are at least eight of them in her growing entourage. She's sweating. Her face is turning the same shade as her pink overalls. The giggling thrums in her ears like rushing water, and it feels like an unseen hand is dunking her head below the surface.

Before she can make sense of what's happening, she's dashed out of the auditorium.

Twenty minutes later, she's exiting the grocery store. She's spent all her lunch money on the missing ingredients for her mom's famous sea-salt chocolate-chip cookies.

Grandma looks up from her morning talk show when Kim comes through the front door. "What are ya doin' home already?"

"I'm sorry, I'm sorry." Kim is sobbing now.

Grandma puts out her cigarette and goes to her. She rubs Kim's back while moving her away from blocking the television. "It's okay, sweetheart. I know you'll be braver tomorrow."

Kim shuffles into the kitchen, sets the grocery bag on the white-tiled counter, and pulls out the stainless-steel measuring cups and mixing bowl.

Grandma follows her. "Dare I ask what's in that bag?"

Kim whispers through her sniffles and a lot of face wiping with the back of her hand, "I need to bake cookies."

Grandma kisses the top of her head before returning to her talk show. "Okay, sweetie. You bake cookies."

Kim's racing heartbeat slows as she measures the ingredients. Her breathing steadies while she mixes the batter. Soon, the cookies are in the oven. She sits on a stool and watches through the small window as they rise.

When the timer buzzes, she takes them out to let them cool on the stovetop. She walks upstairs to her bedroom to change into her favorite pink footsie pajamas. She lies on her bed, wraps the worn strawberry patchwork quilt around her, and waits for the scent of fresh-baked cookies to waft in from downstairs and find her. She closes her eyes and breathes it in, dreaming of her mother in the kitchen and her father reading in the dining room.

She'll try again tomorrow.

There is something about falling asleep after a bad experience. You doze off believing the sting of it will have softened once you awaken. Kim falls for it every time. *"Tomorrow is another day,"* that's what Kim's mom used to say, but then her eyes flash open, and she remembers her parents are dead, and it feels like she's woken up in the wrong life, and the ache that was gone while she slept descends onto her chest once again—an unbearable weight. *Will it always be like this?*

Kim stares at the framed photo of the majorette—her mother, at sixteen—leading the band in the Home Day's parade. She was always at the front of the pack. Kim resolves to go to marching band tryouts next year. She *will* make the band next year.

She falls asleep, dreaming of chocolate and salty air, cotton candy and carousel horses, and the distant sounds of a parade marching down Main Street.

# TWO

It's dark outside. Kim rolls over in bed, and her stomach growls. She's slept through lunch and dinner. She's done it before. Grandma knows not to wake her. Best to leave her be when she gets upset. *"Let her rest,"* she always says. Grandma is nice like that. Jake is another story. He'd shake her awake if he could, but now that he's reunited with his friends, he'll be out all day and night. He doesn't know she ditched today. If he did, he would have come home to read Kim the riot act and told her again how high school isn't like middle school, and she can't go home and bake cookies anytime she feels anxious.

Had the school called to check on her, and if so, what had Grandma told them? Jake doesn't know what anxiety is—he's been the confident one his whole life. At their parents' funeral, he stood in his suit, thirteen years old, and shook the hands of everyone who attended, looking them in the eye, thanking them for coming.

Kim was at his side, unspeaking, a numb doll in her black dress. That was the last time she wore black. Kim hates black.

The strange scraping in the hallway is back, same as last night. She sits up in bed, ready to grab her quilt and dash into the closet. She thinks of Jake calling her life-a-phobic, Grandma telling her to be brave, and her promise to herself to try harder tomorrow.

With shaking limbs, she climbs from bed, snatches her baton, and cracks her bedroom door open. A shadow whisks by. She wants to slam the door shut in terror, but she stops, unable to look away. The shadow flies to the end of the hall and slips inside Grandma's room. Kim considers hiding in her closet and never coming out again. *But what if that thing is about to hurt Grandma?*

Baton held high, ready to swing, Kim tiptoes down the hall. The door to Grandma's room is cracked open, and she peers inside. A hooded figure hovers over Grandma, its bony fingers reaching toward her sleeping form. Grandma's peaceful, steady snores prove she's unaware of the danger.

Kim must act. *This needs to stop!* She can't lose her grandmother. She can't lose anyone else. The bony fingers reach closer, and Grandma's snoring grows erratic, her sleep becoming restless. *It's now or never.*

Something inside Kim snaps. *No, no, no! Leave her alone!* She charges in, bounding onto the bed and leaping at the cowled menace, her baton held high like an assassin's blade. She slams it into the creature's throat. The hooded thing staggers back and claws at its windpipe, gasping, choking. It drops the staff at its side and collapses at the foot of the bed.

The baton falls from Kim's shaking hand and her breath returns in a stuttering, chin-quivering inhale. She hit it. She hit it hard. Had she killed it? Her grandmother's snoring resumes its peaceful rhythm. That woman could sleep through the apocalypse and never stir.

Kim peers over the edge at a heap of black robes on the floor, nothing and no one in sight. Next to the robes is a long staff with a curved blade at one end, its metal catching the moonlight through the window. She recognizes it as a sickle—a tool farmers used to thresh wheat. *What if this thing crawled out of its robes and was now naked under the bed, about to grab its weapon?* Kim has lost the element of surprise, and this creature is enormous, strong, silent, and lightning-fast. She's no match for it now that it knows she's here. Kim snatches the sickle away.

The black robes swirl up as if catching a sudden, strong breeze. They whirl around Kim like a dust devil, enshrouding her. She tries to call out as the robes spin out of control, enveloping her entire frame, but terror hitches the scream in her throat. Kim cries out a name she hasn't spoken in almost five years and vanishes.

All is quiet in the room, save for Grandma's steady, rhythmic snoring.

# Three

Kim is dizzy and the bedroom is spinning. *Wait. This isn't Grandma's room at all.* She stands in an enormous, vaulted cavern on the shoreline of an underground river. Mist swells at her ankles. In the far distance, across the river, a beautiful sunrise glows in vivid lilac, pink, pale yellow, burnt orange, and deep indigo.

The heavy robes enshroud her small frame. The black cowl covers her entire head. She almost finds it cozy for a moment, but she shoves aside the feeling. The robes resist her tugs, as if frozen in place around her head and body.

Kim needs to figure out where she is and how to get home. She grips the sickle with both hands to steady herself. Stabbing its end into the sandy shoreline, she stands hunched to keep her knees from buckling. She strikes a curious pose, like Death incarnate.

Someone or something is watching her. Kim's eyes flash to the river's edge. An ancient man with milky gray eyes and a white beard that reaches his waist stands in a narrow, wooden gondola. He stares in her direction and Kim stares back, unsure of what to say. The man seems to be waiting for something.

"Well?" he asks at last, his voice ragged and deep. "Where is she?"

Kim looks around. She is alone on the shore. "Where's who?"

A perplexed expression crosses the man's wrinkled face, and his beard quivers as he presses his lips together in confusion. "The one you went to get."

Was this man talking about her grandma? "Uh, she couldn't make it."

His confusion turns to annoyance. "What in the blazes does that mean?"

"Yeah, uh, just forget about her. She's not coming." Kim looks around again to ensure they're alone. The man watches her shifty movements, dumbfounded but growing ever more suspicious. "Uh, how do I get back to my house? I have school tomorrow, and I can't miss another day or my brother will kill me."

The man in the gondola scrunches his face as if he's smelled a dead rat. "What are you going on about? House? School? Brother? Did someone hit you over the head? You're Death, you dolt!"

Kim's body goes rigid with fear. "What? No, no, no. I'm not that guy. Nope. No way. I just—I picked up this thing and now…" Kim looks at the sickle, sees the hand holding it is skeletal. *Wait, that's my hand!* She drops the sickle like it's a bag of flaming doggie-doo. It falls onto the sandy shoreline, and the flesh on her hand returns. The black robes swirl and unwind from her body, floating to the ground.

A fifteen-year-old in pink footsie pajamas stands before the ferryman. He stares, mouth agape. In his deadpan, gruff voice, he mutters, "Huzzah," as if Kim has performed a magic trick.

Without her cozy black robes, Kim feels exposed. And frightened. The ferryman shrugs as if accepting her presence as an everyday occurrence. "What's your name, child?"

"Kim. Kim Morse. What's yours?"

"They call me Charon. The boatman."

"Nice to meet you. Am I having a bad dream?"

"Not unless I'm having the same dream, and that seems unlikely."

It makes sense, but what's keeping the people in her dreams from lying to her?

"Tell me, Miss Morse." Charon leans closer to whisper, "Did you *do something* to the person in that black cowl?" He points a gnarled finger toward the robes at Kim's feet.

She doesn't get the sense Charon is angry. He's just curious, so she decides to tell the truth. "I hit him with my majorette baton."

Charon fights back a chuckle. "A baton? Is that so? And, after you did that, did you take up the sickle?"

Kim cringes.

"I see. And after you did that, what did you say?"

"I'm not sure."

"It could be anything, any expression that mentions this place like 'Oh Hell' or 'Heavens to Betsy' or 'Great Hades of the Underworld I bid you good 'morrow.'"

"I called out for Him."

Charon's brow arches. "Him?"

"I said, 'God help me.'"

Charon nods. "That'd do it. Invoking God—or any god—works as an incantation on the Reaper's scythe to transport you here. Any mention of the Afterlife, people, places—"

"Wait, what are you talking about? What is this place? Is that the River Styx? I read about it in one of my dad's books on Greek mythology."

"This is Styx. I am its ferryman. Beyond the river is the Afterlife. And you, my dear, are now the Grim Reaper."

"Nooooo." Kim doesn't know whether to snicker, scream, or sob. The best option might be to sprint but she has no clue where to go.

Charon puffs out a short breath. "Can't help you. It's fate."

Kim shakes her head, her anger rising. "I don't believe in fate."

"Fine. Explain this *situation* in your words."

"I'm having a nightmare."

"Good. Wake up."

Kim pinches her arm. She squeezes her eyes shut, stomps her feet, and screams. The sound echoes through the great cavern.

Charon cracks an almost-smile.

Kim stands with eyes closed and face scrunched from the effort. "I'm still here, aren't I?"

Charon points to the heap at Kim's feet. "Something inside your robes is trying to get your attention."

She opens one eye. A purple glow emits from within the black robes.

"You should check that."

She reaches down with a trembling hand and lifts a foot-tall hourglass from the robes. The purple sand has almost run entirely to the bottom as it pulses with light. "What's this?"

"Your next appointments."

Tiny purple grains fall in slow motion through the narrow end of the hourglass.

"Each grain represents a soul in your world. You need to go collect them as they fall."

"I can't collect all these! I have school tomorrow and cupcakes to bake for the marching band fundraiser."

Charon huffs once. "Try turning it sideways."

Kim cocks her head and turns the hourglass on its side. Everything freezes. Everything but her. She looks at Charon's fixed form and the river's tiny rippling waves frozen at the shoreline. She tilts the hourglass upright again. "I can stop time?"

"To get to each appointment, yes."

Kim considers this newfound power. "Okay, so I stop time. Then what?"

Charon's shoulders slump. *Guess he wasn't prepared to train a newbie tonight?*

The ferryman motions with his hands. "You get the souls. You bring them to me. I take them across the river."

Indignation washes over Kim as she sets down the hourglass. "I'm not gonna go fetch souls for you!"

The ferryman scowls. "They're not for *me*. I'm a shepherd, like you."

"Well, what's across this river?"

Charon cools at this question. "I don't know. I can't leave the boat."

"But...is it, like, Heaven or Hell or what?"

Charon shrugs. "All of it. None of it. No one really knows for sure. Oh, they all pretend to, but they don't. All we know is that if *you* don't go get those dearly departed souls and bring them here, they will wander above for eternity, lost and afraid."

Kim scrunches her nose. "What? Like ghosts?"

"Ghosts, ghouls, specters, spirits—there are many names for them. It happens anytime you fall behind. No matter the names we give them, it all boils down to the same *fate*. These souls risk wandering aimless, growing more paranoid, angrier, and vengeful as time passes, unless *you* bring them home."

"Home? You mean out there?" Kim points to the dark haze and perpetual predawn sunrise across the river. She's tired and afraid, and she's had enough of this crappy dream. "Listen, boatman guy—"

"Charon."

"Yeah, Karen—"

"Cha-ron."

"Charon. Sorry. My parents *had* a home. *You* took them away. Why should I take anyone else from their homes, from their lives, from the people who need them? What if we let everyone live forever? What's wrong with that?"

"It's not for me to explain."

"Well, who can? I wanna talk to them." Kim folds her arms across her chest. She'll get some answers now. She'll make Charon fetch God for her, and they'll sort this out. She's got ideas—better ideas than Him. But Charon isn't moving. *Why does he look sad?*

"Dear child, pick up that sickle and you will discover for yourself."

Kim looks at the sickle, the robes, the hourglass. Her hands drop to her sides. *God isn't coming.* Just like when she got the news about her parents, she cried for Him and begged Him to help, but He never came. "If I do this, will I see my mom and dad again?"

"All loved ones are reunited in the end."

Kim considers the ferryman's words as another grain of purple sand falls. She snatches the sickle in one hand and the hourglass in the other. The black robes swirl around her, and she disappears.

# Four

The Grim Reaper stands before a large building she's never seen before. The sign out front reads *Sunny View Medical Center.* The Grim Reaper hates hospitals.

She pauses, reconsidering. Forget *fate*—she doesn't want to do this. But if she does it, the ferryman says she'll see her parents again. Death needs to be brave. The hourglass she holds tugs at her arm, leading her through the large revolving doors and inside the building.

Death ducks and hides, doing her best to go undetected. She slips into the stairwell. The hourglass leads her to the fourth floor. She creeps down hallways, avoiding the patrolling security guard and the nurses in white making their rounds.

The hourglass halts outside room 401, and the Grim Reaper peers inside. There is a woman, neither old nor young, in the bed. She is asleep with tubes in her nose, down her throat, in her arms. The Reaper wants to cry. This is no way to live. The woman is not getting better, and the Reaper knows this somehow. She also knows she can do something about it, but isn't sure how. Death has always been squeamish around sick people. Touching them is out of the question, but the hourglass is insistent, nudging the Grim Reaper's arm until she relents.

Reaching out, the Reaper marvels at her skeletal hand. The sight of it creeps her out, and she pulls it back under her robes. The hourglass counters with a shove, and her bony fingers propel forward, gently coming to rest on the woman's sternum. A tiny ball of undulating light rises from the woman's chest, floating in front of the Reaper, mesmerizing her.

A droning, high-pitched tone erupts from one of the many devices along the wall, breaking the Reaper's fascination. The blipping green waves in the viewscreen become a steady flatline.

The Reaper panics, looking for a place to hide. She notices the woman standing at the bedside, watching her own prone body in the hospice bed. The woman turns to regard the black-robed figure at her side. She doesn't panic when she sees the Reaper. She seems confused but unafraid. "What do we do? What can we do?"

"It's gonna be okay, be brave," Death says, placing a comforting skeletal hand on the woman's shoulder. Then the Reaper whispers the one phrase she trusts will work: "God help me. "

Her robes expand and swirl around the hospital room, enveloping the woman. A moment passes, and the two arrive dizzy on the shoreline of a great underground river.

The ferryman is there waiting, and the Grim Reaper can tell from the ancient man's expression that he is proud of her. He doesn't speak a word, yet the woman knows to board the gondola. He pushes off the shoreline with his long pole, and they float onto open water.

Death waves, and the sweet, departed soul waves back, free from pain and sorrow. The boat fades into the cavernous dark, and the woman becomes a point of light. As the ferryman rows deeper into the fog, that point of light diffuses to a hazy glow. Another purple grain of sand slips through the narrow center of the hourglass, tugging at the Reaper's arm, beckoning the cycle to begin again.

The Reaper will make eight more trips in the next half-hour. There will be three more hospital visits to countries and continents she has not visited before. There's no time to sightsee. Most souls are old, but some are young. Some died in a flash of unfortunate trauma, while some left the world after a slow and debilitating decline. The Reaper is not sure which way is worse or better. She decides fast must be better, even if it comes too soon, like the way her parents went. She hopes they felt no pain.

Death finds it strange how her clothes and features transform as she travels through different regions. In Southern Asia, her black robes shift to colorful hues. In certain parts of Africa, she loses them altogether and becomes a walking skeleton—*kinda embarrassing*—while in others, her robes transmute into a glossy wax-coated cotton with beautiful prints in bright, bold colors. In Mexico, she wears this over-the-top, wide-brimmed hat with flowers. *It's super-chic.* She grows wings in Eastern Europe and boar tusks in Japan, but her job remains the same everywhere she travels: collect souls and bring them to the ferryman.

On Death's ninth trip, a nine-year-old girl in a white cotton dress stands beside an overturned automobile on an empty two-lane highway in New Mexico. The police have yet to arrive. The girl in white is afraid. She thinks her family has forgotten her. *Why is she alone?* The Reaper peers inside the overturned car. There are four people inside. All unconscious. Three of them are breathing. The fourth is the body of the girl who stands alone on this desolate highway. The Reaper reaches out a skeletal hand and touches the child, who does not move.

Death hates the sight of blood, so she turns away. She does not want the child to see herself, so she takes her for frozen yogurt a few miles up the road. The shop is closed, but that does not matter. The Reaper tells the girl she can sample any flavor, but she asks for cookies and cream and no others. Death understands. It's her favorite flavor, too.

The two sit under the starry night, eating their frozen yogurt. Once the girl has had her fill, she takes the Reaper's hand, and they travel to see the ferryman. Once there, the girl climbs aboard, and the Reaper watches the gondola as it fades into the distance. The girl becomes a bright point of light before diffusing into the misty dark.

Death will never forget her.

After collecting souls for half the night, the Grim Reaper stands in a narrow alleyway in what she thinks is Mumbai. She doesn't know how she knows this, but she's correct. The sun is already shining and there is the wafting scent of cooking spices and aromatic herbs. The ground is wet, and the high walls of the encroaching buildings are dilapidated. It is Death's first appointment during daylight hours. The heat and humidity are oppressive—a hectic, bustling city swarms ahead where the alley meets the street.

The Reaper takes a tentative step forward and notices she is no longer in black robes but in bright gold and blue robes. She freezes. How can she remain undetected in the daytime in a busy city? She turns the hourglass sideways, and the city sounds cease. Nothing moves, not even the laundry hanging from the line three stories above her.

The Reaper takes another step and pauses. The hourglass isn't showing her the way when it's sideways. How does she do this? She looks around. A huddled figure lies in a dark enclave. Lack of food has withered their limbs and prolonged exposure to the sun has browned their paper-thin skin. Death peers closer, and though this man's sunken eyes are closed and his face gaunt, he is smiling. The Reaper cannot help but smile, too. She touches his chest and whispers, "Om Shanti." She does not know where the words come from and isn't even certain what they mean, but she feels it's the right thing to say.

A hand rests on Death's shoulder, and she almost jumps out of her robes. She turns and the man's soul stands at her side. His grin widens and laughs with amusement. He speaks, and to her surprise, she understands his words. "Oh, to surprise great Yama himself, what a treat. You have come to take me to my next life, no doubt. Let us leave this place. Where is your horse?"

The Reaper speaks in a language she's never uttered until today. "Um, mai bhool gaya."

The man erupts with a deep belly laugh. "Oh Yama, forgotten your horse? Such humor you have."

The man does not look hungry, old, or tired anymore. He is joyful, as if ready to embark on a great adventure. The Reaper takes his hand and whispers, "God help me." They appear at the river's edge, where Charon awaits.

The exuberant man bounds toward the gondola, hugging the ferryman the instant he steps aboard. Charon remains silent as he pushes off the shoreline and sets his boat adrift.

The Reaper sets down her sickle, and the robes unwind to reveal a teenage girl in fuzzy pink pajamas. The man sees Kim on the shoreline where the Hindu god of death stood moments ago. He laughs again, a great big guffaw of glee. "Oh, Yama, how you surprise me in return!"

Kim calls to Charon. "When will you be back? I have questions!"

Charon nods but gives no indication of how long he will be away. The boat fades into the misty dark as the man's joyful soul loses its earthly form and becomes a bright point of light.

Kim paces the sandy shore until Charon's gondola reemerges from the mist and comes to a soft stop at the river's edge.

"Okay, first—why don't you ever talk when I bring you souls? You never say a word. How 'bout a 'hey, welcome in' or something?"

Charon strokes his white beard as he regards Kim with a withering expression. "Do you have any idea how many questions they ask—for the entire journey across the river—once they learn I can talk? They're relentless. *Where are we going? What's on the other side? How long will it take? When do I get to meet my wife, my brother, my father, what's his name and so-and-so?* No, thank you. Better to have them believe I'm a mute."

"Wow. Okay, I can kinda get that. Next question: Aren't you supposed to be taking coins from all these people? Y'know, 'pay the ferryman' and all that?"

Charon clenches his jaw, holding in an outburst. "Ehh, yes, the coin thing. This ritual stems from a time when people left dead bodies out to rot. The coins were a way to encourage people to inter their dead with respect. However, the notion that I collect these coins conveys that none but the rich may attain the Afterlife. The idea is preposterous. Where would I spend it? I can't leave the boat. And what of the poor children bagged and thrown in a lake? Should I deny them passage?"

Kim is appalled. "No! Gads, that's dark."

"It's the world, child. There is much darkness to overcome." Charon nods to the hourglass. "You keep bringing me souls, no matter their condition or wealth, and rest assured, I will take them across. So quit lollygagging on the shoreline."

"Yeah, that's my other question: how am I supposed to get everywhere unseen? It's weird sneaking all over the place, not to mention impossible in broad daylight."

Charon's face scrunches up like he's sniffed month-old beans hiding in the back of his refrigerator. "Why are you sneaking around? Nobody can see you!"

"What?! All this time you've got me hiding in stairwells and creeping along dark passages, and now you're saying no one can see me?"

"I didn't tell you to do that."

"Well, how come *I* saw me? I mean, how did I see the Grim Reaper when he stood over my grandma?"

Charon's lips go tight and bloodless. "Hmm. You've got a ghost."

"I have a what?"

"If a spirit attaches itself to you, then you could maybe, *possibly*, see Death."

"Um, okay. So why can't I see this ghost now?"

"Most spirits anchor themselves to a specific place, like your home."

"So you're saying my house is haunted?"

"Have you been home since becoming, um," he motions to the robes and scythe lying at Kim's feet, "that guy?"

"I've only been where this hourglass takes me."

"Well, you can sort out the ghost thing when you go back for your grandmother's soul."

Kim gasps in alarm. "What? I'm not bringing my grandma to you!"

Charon juts his bottom lip and nods. "I see. You'd rather she become a ghoul."

"A ghoul?"

"A zombie, a ghast, an undead walking the earth."

"You're kidding."

Charon fixes Kim with a sobering glare. *He's not kidding.* The blood drains from Kim's face. She might vomit. "C'mon, Charon, you know I can't do it." She's whining and hates the sound of it, but something this serious warrants such a tone.

Charon's voice stays cool. "It must be done."

"Well, then why can't you go get her? Please. Just this one time."

"I already told you, I never leave the boat."

Kim groans and stamps a pink footsie heel on the sandy shore. She's being petulant, but she doesn't care. "Ughhh! This job sucks. When can I quit?"

"I'm not sure you can, and I must say, you are falling *woefully behind.*"

Kim looks at the massive hourglass resting at her feet, the purple grains dropping one by one. She wants to kick it. "Well, I'm sorry. Maybe when the folks around here realize I'm no good at this job, they'll come by so I can explain the whole mix-up and get it fixed."

Charon smooths his beard as if considering the idea. "Erm, maybe best not to meet those folks. I have a hunch they will be none too pleased by your presence."

"Ughhh!" Kim throws her arms in the air, exasperated. The outburst reminds her of one of Jake's signature moves, and it annoys her even more that she did it.

"If it's any consolation, I think you're making a pretty good go of it."

Kim narrows her eyes, suspicion rising. "Me? You think I'm good at being Death?"

"Well, you've brought me only a dozen so far, but they all seemed quite content, not afraid or crying. They came willingly, yes?"

"I mean, yeah, but—"

"You made them feel safe. That counts for something. It takes a big heart to shine through those heavy black robes, my dear. You're off to a smashing start."

"Oh. Well, thanks. That was a nice thing to say, I guess. But how do I catch up? That last guy said I'm supposed to have a horse."

Charon's face brightens. "Oh right, the horse! It's in your robes somewhere. Check the pockets."

"There's a horse inside my robes...in a pocket?" Kim falls to her knees in the sand and begins rummaging through the black robes. She feels something cool and hard. Her hand emerges, holding a white marble figurine. It's a carved horse the size of a dinner roll. "Is this a joke?"

"There are no jokes in the Underworld. That's your mighty steed!"

The marble figurine hits the ground, sending up a spray of sand. Kim groans. It's her fourth attempt to summon her *mighty steed*, but it's not working.

Charon watches from the boat, looking glum. "Try it again. I think your accent is off."

Kim grimaces. "Well, I'm sure it is. I've never spoken *Latin* before."

"You'll get it. The last guy had an eternity to master the nuances."

"Ehhh, I can't!" Kim knows she needs to stop whining, but it can't be helped. "This is stupid! I'm falling further behind with every passing second. Maybe I don't need the stupid horse?"

"She'll never show if you keep calling her stupid."

Kim pauses. "It's a girl horse?"

"I believe they're called mares. And yes, Death rides a pale mare."

Kim's intrigue grows. "What's her name?"

Charon strokes his beard. "Ah, I don't know that she has one."

"Seriously? Who doesn't name their horse?"

Charon raises his hand. "The Grim Reaper! What do I win?"

Kim smirks. "You don't win anything."

Charon looks put out. "But I gave the correct answer."

"Even so."

The ferryman leans into his long pole and exhales a great sigh. "Well, then I guess there's nothing left to do but try again. It's either that or quit, and we're not quitters around here." Charon watches Kim from the corner of his eye, hopeful she won't give up.

Kim gnaws at her lower lip. She bends to pick up the marble horse and tosses it again, exclaiming, "Vita mutator, non tollitur!"

The figurine lands in a spray of sand. It lies on its side, a single carved eye peering at her as if to say, *'YoU cAn'T dO It.'* Kim stomps her fuzzy pink foot in frustration.

"No, no, no." Charon waves his hands. "First you say it, then you throw it."

"Last time you said I wasn't throwing it fast enough!"

"You weren't. Try again."

Kim lifts the figurine and readies to throw.

"Wait!"

Kim pauses, arm raised overhead.

Charon leans closer and whispers. "Don't *say* the words. *Believe* them."

Kim rolls her eyes and drops her arm to her side. "Oh, sure, because I know Latin. What am I even saying? I have no idea!"

Charon does his best to stand straight and proud. He's about to say something profound. Kim can tell it's the secret she's been waiting for. "*Vita mutator, non tollitur:* Life is changed, not taken away. It means that death *transforms* life. It is not the end of life. The soul is eternal. It goes on, never-ending."

Kim has never been more let down by a moment of profundity. "So dead people don't stop living. Is that seriously what you're saying?"

"Well. No, not quite." Charon points a gnarled finger at Kim. "Your body is a miracle. It is! Your life started as one tiny egg and one microscopic sperm and a trillion chemical reactions later—a trillion over a mere forty weeks, no time at all—out you came, a brand-new baby. If that's not a miracle, I don't know what is! And you continue to grow and change every day. You're in a state of constant transformation. Why should that change in death? No, it is not the *end*. It is another miracle change, beyond our comprehension."

Kim considers Charon's words. "Of all the things I didn't think I'd be doing tonight, getting a Sex Ed lecture from a centenarian was the thing I expected least."

Charon's face scrunches up as if he's eaten an olive thinking it was a grape. "Who the heck is Sexy Ed?"

"It's not a person. You know what? Never mind." Kim raises the horse again. She thinks of her parents as not dead. Not gone. Just some place different, still living, only not with her, or maybe not where she can *see* them. Her heart aches and brightens, almost as if it's expanding in two directions, and perhaps this is what she needs to feel. "Vita mutator, non tollitur!" she exclaims and throws down the horse.

A spray of shaved ice erupts into the air, leaving a thin layer of hoarfrost on Kim's cheeks. Her body shivers with a mix of biting cold and tingling excitement.

A towering, pale mare emerges from the frosty mist. The horse has a bone-white, gray-marbled, almost translucent coat. Her silver mane and tail are luxurious, wavy, and long. She shakes her head once, sending frosty dew in all directions. Eyes like frozen ponds regard the girl in the fuzzy pink pajamas with placid acceptance, awaiting her instruction.

"Huzzah," Charon mutters, but Kim can tell he's impressed. She, however, is at a total loss for words. She's never seen a more beautiful creature.

Kim recalls museum paintings from master artists depicting Death's horse as an old nag, ribs showing, swaybacked, haggard. This is not that horse. She reaches out and strokes the pink nose, and it's like resting her hand against a perfect snowball. "You're magnificent."

The horse whinnies low and stomps her foot twice in anticipation. Kim retrieves her sickle. Black robes swirl and enshroud her, lifting her onto the mare's back in one graceful motion. Death raises her hourglass, watches as another purple grain of sand drops. "Let's go."

Death rides a pale horse through the brooding predawn fog, her black-robed silhouette basking in the dim purple light of a foot-tall hourglass. She's been awake all night collecting souls for the ferryman to take across the river lest they become ghosts roaming the land.

When the sun breaks on the eastern horizon, the Grim Reaper leaves the shoreline of an underground river, turns her mighty steed into a small marble figurine, and heads home after a long night's work.

With the hourglass as her guide, Death returns to her grandmother's bedroom. The house is dark, and she checks on Grandma, who snores as if nothing can disturb her. She tiptoes down the hall and peers into Jake's room. He's sleeping as well. If they woke, would they see her? And where is this *supposed ghost* that helped her to see the Reaper?

Kim shakes off all the questions, too tired to solve any more riddles. She whisks to her bedroom to hide the scythe in her closet. The robes swirl and unfurl from her body, leaving her standing once more in pink footsie pajamas. She feels like herself again, but also different. She takes long, slow breaths, in and out once, twice, trying to make sense of the evening's events.

It's 5:22 in the morning. She needs to be up soon for school but hasn't slept all night.

Kim tips the hourglass on its side and sets it on the nightstand. Time stops, save for her. The sky outside freezes, and the waking birds cease their chirping. True quiet. Too quiet. Kim climbs into bed, reaches for her phone, and puts in her earbuds. She listens to her favorite song on repeat and runs her slideshow of family memories until she falls fast asleep.

She awakes to discover she hasn't slept so well in almost five years. The sunrise is still in the same spot on the horizon, and there are no sounds. She tips the hourglass upright, and the whole world churns awake like a giant carousel coming to life. The birds chirp, the breeze blows the leaves in the trees, and a car rumbles down her street. Kim hears her grandmother's low snoring from the end of the hall. Jake yawns. *Time to face the music.*

High school day two, the do-over edition, and this time, Kim has got this thing in the bag. She is R-E-A-D-Y, ready. She's picked out her outfit, pre-packed her lunch, and put together individual bags of fresh-baked sea-salt chocolate-chip cookies for her teachers—*now that's how you introduce yourself!* Sure, marching band tryouts have come and gone, along with orientation, finding her locker and her classrooms and the cafeteria, and doing her day-one assignments and homework, and making new friends, or any friends, and—*Oh, no. Ohhh, noooo. It's never going to work.*

"Hey." Jake leans against the door and pokes his head into the bedroom. "You're already dressed and ready. Radical improvement from yesterday, sis. Good job."

Kim's face drains of color. Her lower lip trembles. "I can't go."

Jake huffs and rolls his eyes. "Kimmy! C'mon!"

Kim shakes her head. "I, uh, I can't, I'm serious. I'm so far behind in my high school experience, I'll never catch up. Never!"

Jake arches a brow. "It's been one day. How are you behind?"

Kim freezes. Her brother doesn't know she left before orientation. It needs to stay that way. He can never find out. Which means she has to go to school and get caught up. If she doesn't, Jake will murder her.

Fear is a funny thing. Kim knows this. One of the last pieces of advice that her dad ever gave her was: "Anytime you're afraid to do something, tell yourself something even more terrifying will happen if you *don't* do that thing you're afraid of, and it will kick your butt into gear so fast, people will think you're the most confident person in the room."

When faced with *going to school* vs. *death by brother*, the choice for Kim is clear. She lifts her star unicorn backpack and hurries downstairs.

Grandma is at the kitchen table. No coffee, no toast, and no cigarette. The *no cigarette* part is good, but she looks pasty pale and a bit hazy, moving slower, too.

Kim toasts two cinnamon apple tarts for herself before heading for the door.

"Have a good day at school," Grandma says.

*That's a good sign.* Kim kisses her on the cheek. Grandma smells weird, like she hasn't showered in days. *Might need to mention it if it gets any worse.*

A few minutes later, Kim is in the backseat of her brother's car with his loud friends. She is on the way to high school, day two: the do-or-die edition.

# Eight

Kim finds her locker and her homeroom with her English teacher, Mrs. Bell—a woman in her sixties with dyed black hair and intense green eyes. Kim thinks there is a strong possibility Mrs. Bell doesn't believe in unicorns, mermaids, or even rainbows. When Kim gives her a plate of chocolate-chip cookies, the woman does not look pleased or say thank you. She stares at them like they're a dish of fresh cat turds and asks if they contain gluten. Kim did not add gluten. She's never even heard of that ingredient. Flour, butter, eggs, sea salt, chocolate chips—they're made with real stuff. She tells Mrs. Bell there is no gluten.

Kim's not sure she likes Mrs. Bell as she scuttles away to find an empty seat. She sets down her binder and notices Taylor sitting two desks over. Kim groans, but on the inside. Taylor is pretending she doesn't see

Kim, who decides to act like she does not see Taylor. But Kim *totally* sees Taylor. Even when she looks at the whiteboard at the front of the room, she can feel Taylor over her left shoulder—*staring.*

When she can't take it anymore, she glances over to catch Taylor watching, but...Taylor is not. It's someone else looking Kim's way. Who is this girl dressed all in black, with long dark hair and severe bangs, three nose piercings, heavy black eyeliner, and a t-shirt with the word "Misfits" on it? What kind of person announces they're a misfit right on their shirt?

Kim squints, envisioning giving this girl a proper makeover with rainbow barrettes and pink lipstick. Scary Goth Girl would be cute if she learned the value of color, and maybe—*oh crap!* Goth Girl is still intensely staring, and now they're staring *at each other.*

Kim whips her gaze away and fixates on the front of the room, panicked that Goth Girl caught her ogling. What if this girl retaliates? What if she calls her a baby? *Wait. She started it!* When she steals a peek over her shoulder all casual-like, Goth Girl hasn't budged. Kim turns away. Something bounces off the back of her head—a folded paper on the floor. She bends to pick it up, unfolds it, and reads the heavy black ink:

*Meet me after class. Gwyn. xxx*

*Oh crap.* Going to school was supposed to be better than getting murdered by Jake, but now she's going to get murdered by Scary Goth Girl Gwyn. *This is the worst.*

*Wait a minute—who would come and collect her soul if she died? Can she die?* She needs to ask Charon about this potential major loophole.

Mrs. Bell assigns *The Picture of Dorian Gray* by Oscar Wilde as the class's first book report. Kim is looking forward to it. A book about a guy who never grows old and lives forever sounds right up her alley.

English ticks by like slow-motion grains of sand in an hourglass, and she counts the seconds until the end of class. She plans on sprinting to the principal's office before Goth Gwyn catches her.

The bell rings. Kim darts from her desk, speed-walking down the aisle, but—oh no, Finley Mavet is blocking her way. Kim knows Fin from middle school. Her name always comes after his during roll call. *"Mavet." "Here!" "Morse." "Present!"*

Finley is even more formidable than a year ago— over six feet tall and at least three hundred pounds. He moves like—well, Kim doesn't want to say or even think the words *rolling refrigerator,* but she can't help it. Finley turns her way.

"Oh. Hey, Kim. How was your summer?"

"Great, Fin. Hope yours was great, too. Gotta go, 'scuse me." Kim scoots around him as he hoists his backpack over his shoulder.

"Oh, sure, no worries," Fin says as Kim squeezes past. She knows she's being rude. Fin's always been nice to her, but this is a life-or-death situation. Kim sprints for the door and stops short. Gwyn stands in the doorway, arms folded across her chest, waiting.

*Uh-oh. Time to die.*

Kim's face drains of color. She gives one of those big fake smiles with a short wave. "Oh, hey. Uh, got your note."

Gwyn grabs Kim's teal sweatshirt—the one with the airbrushed mermaids—and yanks her from the doorway so their classmates can pass. As Gwyn does this, Kim feels light-headed, expecting to have her head slammed against a locker and her lights punched out.

It doesn't happen.

Gwyn lets go of the sweater and adjusts the rainbow barrette in Kim's hair. "So, hey, you seem like a person who likes colors."

Kim blinks. She *is* a person who likes colors, but she's not sure if this is a trick question or not.

Gwyn narrows her eyes. "Are you or are you not?"

Kim nods. "Uh-huh."

"Cool." Gwyn relaxes her shoulders. "So, have you ever dyed your hair? Like purple or magenta or anything?"

Kim has *not* dyed her hair. She has always *wanted* to dye her hair, but her parents wouldn't allow it. Of course, now that they're dead, maybe Kim is free to do what she likes with her hair...but they had been so against it, Kim feels like she'd be going behind their backs if she *did* dye her hair, and so Kim *can't* dye her hair, not until she's at least eighteen or—

"Hey!" Gwyn gives Kim a little shove. "Where'd you go?"

"Oh, sorry."

"It's a simple yes or no. It's not like I'm asking you to solve for X of anything."

"Oh, uh, sorry. Yeah, no, I've never dyed my hair, sorry."

"Stop apologizing." Gwyn looks annoyed. "So, you've never dyed your hair?"

Kim shakes her head. "No, sor— I mean, no?"

Gwyn frowns. "Okay, then." She turns to go but stops when Taylor Mead bumps into her.

Taylor doesn't acknowledge Gwyn, but she *does* notice Kim. "Hey, little baby," she croons as she walks. Kim's face goes hot, and she thinks her cheeks may have turned crimson.

Gwyn scowls, lifting her middle finger as if proud to show off her chipped black nail polish. "Sit and spin, fatty."

All the color drains from Kim's face.

Taylor stops cold and looks over her shoulder, eyes wide and mouth agape. She huffs a high whine like a broken tea kettle before storming down the hall.

Kim can't believe what she just heard—*Scary Goth Girl Gwyn told off Taylor Mead.*

"It's not nice to body shame," Kim says before she can stop herself. After what she was thinking about Finley Mavet moments earlier, she's one to talk, but still.

Gwyn scoffs. "Who cares? She's a stuck-up little brat."

Kim agrees with the second part but isn't sure about the first part. "I mean, even so, it's not nice. We can't be friends if you talk bad about people."

Gwyn folds her arms across her Misfits t-shirt. She seems to like this stance. "Who says I wanted to be friends?"

"Oh," Kim fumbles, unsure. "Then, uh, why did you want to talk to me right now? I mean, about colors and stuff."

Gwyn looks away and bites her lower lip like she wants to say something but doesn't know how to say it. "I'm new here. It's just me and my mom, who's a real *b-i-t-c-h* if you catch my subtle meaning. Basically, I don't know anybody and have no friends, but I wanted to dye my hair after school and I got this hair color from the store: Midnight Ruby. You seemed like someone who could maybe help me, y'know, with the back and stuff. And if you did, I could help you dye your hair after we did mine. Whatever color you wanted. Electric blue would look cute on you, but I guess you're not into that, so whatever, it's cool." Gwyn turns to go.

"Hey, hold up!" A lightning-flash tingles through Kim's entire body as she blurts out the words. Gwyn pauses and looks back. "Let's do it."

*Did I just say that?* She's going to dye her hair even though her parents said no. But that was years ago, and she's wanted blue and pink streaked hair since she was nine.

Gwyn flashes a crooked grin. "Oh? Okay, cool. Meet me in the quad after school. We'll go to the store to pick out your color. We might need some bleach, too."

"Cool." Kim's cheeks are glowing. She's smiling— no, she's beaming. *Okay, day two of high school. Not so awful.*

Gwyn leans in close. "One thing you should know about me, I mean, if we're gonna be *friends*...I can be kinda judgy. I'm working on it, but when I see how most people live in constant fear—instead of celebrating life—it pisses me off. Fear only makes people into two things: timid or mean."

Kim wonders if that's true and recalls her father's advice. "I think fear can also be a great motivator, sometimes."

"I guess if you've got a pack of wolves chasing you, maybe you're more motivated to run for your life?" Gwyn huffs, unconvinced. "But it takes a special kind of person to take all their fears and turn them into something kind and good in the world."

The bell rings. Kim lifts her star unicorn backpack to leave. "Gotta get to class. Meet you later in the quad."

"Later." Gwyn struts off. *Do I look that cool when I walk?* Scary Goth Girl Gwyn moves like a prowling leopard. Kim tends to bounce on the balls of her feet, more like a frolicking fawn than a hunting cat. She heads to her next class, thinking about how she walks and trying to add some prowl to her steps as she goes.

# Nine

There are, like, one hundred thousand kids in the quad after school, Kim's sure of it. She will never find Gwyn in this sea of failing AXE body spray, Eilish No. 2, and teen angst. This place needs the scent of fresh-baked cookies something fierce. She covers her nose and waits.

"Hey."

The whisper startles Kim and she spins a half-circle. Gwyn smells like black licorice and clove smoke. Kim likes it. *It's important in a friendship,* she thinks while hoping she still smells like her bubblegum body wash, but she's concerned she smells like teenage perspiration after the day she's had.

"Oh, hey," she says, relieved that Gwyn hasn't stood her up. "So, which store are we going to?"

"The pharmacy on Seventh, but these shoes kinda suck for walking."

Gwyn is wearing five-inch platform, lace-up, knee-high boots. They look like something a witch from the future would wear.

"My brother can maybe give us a ride?" Kim offers.

"Who's your brother?"

Kim points toward the parking lot. Jake is there with Danny and Brian, tossing a football and chatting with the cheerleading squad as they walk by in tight formation.

"That guy?" Gwyn raises an eyebrow. "Well hello, new boytoy."

"Hey! I said that's my brother."

"Oh, right. He seems like a *promising young man.*"

Kim and Gwyn exchange a look as if waiting for the other to crack. Kim breaks first. "So? Are we asking him for a ride or what?"

"Heck yeah, babe."

Kim bristles. *Babe isn't the same as baby, is it? No. It isn't.* Okay. Gwyn can call her babe. It's cool. The girls walk side-by-side to the parking lot.

"We need a ride to the pharmacy," Kim announces.

"Pshh," Jake scoffs. "What am I, your taxi service?"

"Jakob." Kim does her best impersonation of her mother. "Help your sister."

"Pfff!" He huffs and shakes his head. "Whatever." He reaches into his pocket to retrieve his keys while jutting his chin in Gwyn's direction. "Who's this?"

Gwyn smirks. "Me?" She throws an arm around Kim. "I'm her new best friend."

Jake scrutinizes Gwyn. "Is that right?"

"Yep," Kim says, going along but also unconvinced. Is she Gwyn's best friend? Does Gwyn even know her actual name? She keeps referring to Kim as *you* and *her* and *babe*.

"Does your new best friend have a name?" Jake asks.

Gwyn holds out her hand. "I'm Gwyn."

Jake frowns at the outstretched hand with its chipped polish. A devilish grin creeps up his face as he holds out his arms. "I'm a hugger."

Kim shoves her brother and grabs Gwyn by the arm, leading her toward the car door. "Nope! Let's go."

Jake grins. "Sure thing, sis."

As the girls climb into the backseat, Gwyn leans close to whisper, "Kinda wanted a hug, you killjoy."

"Not on my watch." The two giggle and it soon turns to unbridled laughter—they can't stop.

Jake looks at them through the rearview mirror. "What's so hysterical back there?"

The girls continue laughing. They're not even sure why anymore, but they can't contain themselves. "Nothing!"

Jake starts the car. "Weirdos."

# Ten

The girls stand in aisle five, staring at hair dye. Should she? Should she not? Kim picks out Blue Ruin and Atomic Pink Floss. "These."

Gwyn nods. "Those." She grabs them and puts one dye in each pocket of her khaki green denim jacket.

A cold rush of anxiety washes over her. "Wait, what are you doing?" *Is Gwyn planning to steal hair dye?*

"Oh? Did you bring money?" Gwyn wonders aloud.

Kim looks aghast. "Yeah, I brought money. I babysit, like, three nights a week. I have money."

"Ew. Kids suck."

Kim nods. "I know. They're the worst. Which is why spending my hard-earned cash is so gratifying." She snatches the dye out of Gwyn's pockets.

Gwyn smirks. "Fine, have it your way." She picks up a hair bleach kit. "Got enough for this too? Those colors won't take if you don't go platinum first."

Kim bites her lip as she adds up the prices. "Crap. Do you have some extra cash?"

"Nope. I don't have *any* money."

Kim scrunches her nose, considering both hair dyes. She takes the pink jar and tries to return it on the shelf, but Gwyn slaps her hand away. "Ow! Hey!"

"You are *not* putting that back. You want two colors and you're gonna get two colors."

"How? I don't have enough for Blue Ruin and Atomic Pink Floss plus the bleach." Kim's voice goes extra quiet. "And we're not shoplifting. I'm serious."

"How short are you?" Gwyn asks.

"I'm five-foot-one," Kim replies, unsure how that relates to the conversation and tensing for a short-person joke at her expense.

Gwyn fights a laugh. "I meant, how much *money* are you short?"

"Oh!" Kim giggles. "Like two dollars, maybe?"

"Oh, this is easy." Gwyn takes the bleach kit and hair dyes and struts toward the checkout.

Kim whisper-hisses, "Gwyn! I don't have—" She glowers as she follows her new best friend to the register.

The cashier scans the items and reads the total in a monotone drawl. "That'll be $42.19."

Kim feels her cheeks warm as she pulls out two twenty-dollar bills. "I only have $40."

The cashier stares at the forty dollars. "It's $42.19"

Gwyn leans across the register and glances at the cashier's name tag. "Hey, Jemma? Listen, my friend here *really* needs this hair dye. We've been planning a makeover for her all week. There's this guy at school. Total hottie. She's head over heels for him but she's, like, invisible to this guy because boys are morons, am I right? Anyway, she needs to get his attention. Make a statement. Because this is *real*, Jemma. You believe in true love, don't you? You were a teenage girl once. You know. So, can we have the stuff? I swear, we'll come back tomorrow with the two dollars and nineteen cents. You have our word. But my friend has to get her hair done *to-night*. Don't deny a girl her destiny over two dollars and nineteen cents, Jemma. You don't want to be the woman who stood in the way of true love."

The cashier stares at Gwyn. The girls stare back. No one moves for a full minute until the middle-aged man waiting in line to buy an energy drink clears his throat.

The cashier puffs out her cheeks and sighs. "Ah, screw it. I don't got time for this crap today." She takes the forty dollars and bags the hair dye and bleach.

"Thank you sooo much!" Kim is beaming. She can't believe that worked.

"You're a rock star, Jemma," Gwyn says, raising her fist. "Girl power!"

"Uh-huh. Next customer!"

As they head for the sliding doors, Gwyn leans in and bumps her shoulder against Kim's shoulder. "Sometimes you gotta ask for what you want. Otherwise, you spend your whole life doing whatever everybody else wants."

Charon waits in his boat, leaning against his staff. It's been hours since the Grim Reaper has brought him any souls. She's falling behind. Way behind. It's bad, and Charon knows it. He worries about what the world is coming to now that the sickle is in the hands of a teenage girl. Does it portend the End Times? No, he does not believe in such myths. He's heard talk of the world's end for eons, and it's never amounted to anything.

Still, if the others catch wind of Death's recent replacement, they'll come calling. He needs to help the girl, "show her the ropes" as they say—what few ropes he knows. It's more like frayed kite strings. He grips his staff tighter, feeling untethered by all the recent changes.

"Is qviet day, boatman?"

Charon's head jerks at the voice. A middle-aged man on a gaunt, swaybacked white stallion saunters closer. His white-stubbled hair, ice-blue eyes, and clean-shaven, pock-scarred face carry an air of impending doom. He's dressed in the pale green robes of a surgeon, though he holds a modern composite bow. A pale green mist wafts from the quiver of arrows at his side.

"M-Martin?" Charon stutters. "L-Lovely to see you. Yes, another pleasant day in paradise, it seems."

The white rider brings his horse closer until its forelegs make small ripples at the river's edge. Small fish float to the surface, bellies upturned. The man leans forward, his face inches from Charon's, who instinctively leans away.

"Vhere iz ze Reaper?" Martin's voice is clipped and suspicious, signaling the repressed rage hiding behind his dead eyes and unreadable expression.

Charon tries to formulate an answer that will appease the Horseman of Pestilence. He does not want to tell Martin where Death is, but he needs to tell him *something* or suspicions will continue to grow.

Martin runs a hand over his white-stubbled head and flicks away a few droplets of sweat. He coughs once—a raspy, phlegmy rattle—and makes no attempt to cover his mouth. He turns his head sideways, places a white-gloved finger over one nostril, and shoots out a stream of snot. It lands on the ledge of Charon's boat and trickles down the side into the water.

He returns his gaze to Charon, his face void of emotion. "I ask you a qvestion, boatman."

Charon plays it cool. "Obviously, the Reaper is out. I'm sure it's a testament to your recent handiwork. Lots of souls to collect." Charon knows the value of praise. He needs to appease Martin and send him away. If he aggravates him, the man will return with the others. That would be bad.

A self-satisfied smirk creeps up Martin's face, but it does not reveal his rotted teeth, nor does it reach his eyes. "Yes, zis latest strain iz qvite deadly. My best vurk in a century."

"A-ha, well, good job." Charon pats the horse's muzzle, trying to come off as nonchalant. His hand is shaking, and he hopes Martin does not notice or, if he does, chalks it up to old age. "I'll be sure to tell Death you stopped by."

Martin regards Charon with his dead-eyed stare. "You do zat, boatman. Tell them Luki and Peggy vant a vurd as vell." The rider turns his horse, and they walk along the shoreline until they disappear into the mist.

Charon strokes his white beard and breathes a heavy sigh. "Well, poop."

# TWeLVe

Gwyn's room is a celebration of all things dark and foreboding. Posters of Bauhaus and The Cure (and other bands Kim has never heard of) adorn the black walls. There is a wolf skull on her dresser and a gargoyle doorstop that leads to her red-tiled bathroom.

Kim stares at her reflection in the bathroom mirror, admiring her new pink- and turquoise-striped hair. She touches it, then runs her fingers through it to confirm it's real. *This is so freakin' weird.* She turns her head from one side to the other, taking in the radical transformation. It's as if she's become a character pulled from her wildest imagination. Also, she admits to looking a bit like her bedroom walls.

"You look so freakin' cool," Gwyn says as she blow-dries her dark blood-red locks. "You're like an insane candy princess from some futuristic fantasy video game."

Kim laughs. "I don't even recognize myself!"

Gwyn shuts off the dryer. "Oh shit, are your parents gonna freak? I'm not getting you in trouble, am I? I swear, if they say we can't hang out anymore, I'm gonna be—"

Kim grabs Gwyn's arm to stop the goth girl from spinning out. "No, no. It's fine. That's, uh, that's not gonna happen."

Gwyn relaxes. "Okay. So your parents are cool. That's a relief."

"Ummm." Kim is not sure what to say or how to say it. Jake always says that the truth is best, but it never comes out how Jake would say it when Kim tells it. But this is her new best friend, Gwyn. She'll understand. *Maybe.*

"My parents died." Kim blurts out the words, then winces when she sees Gwyn's confused expression. Her puzzled look makes Kim anxious—so anxious that she has a sudden case of diarrhea of the mouth. "Yeah, um, so it happened a while ago, I mean, it feels like yesterday sometimes, but it's been, like, almost five years, or more like four years, seven months, and twenty-two days if you want to get technical. It was all over the local news, like a whole thing, and so now my brother and I live with our grandmother. I mean, she lived with us before our patents died, but now she's, like, our guardian. And so, yeah, it sucks they're gone, and I miss them all the time, but no, they won't care at all that I've dyed my hair in crazy pink and blue stripes because—*HA!*—like I said, they're gone. I mean, they died."

The air in the room stills. It reminds Kim of those moments when she's turned the hourglass sideways and the whole world stops. *Oh crap, the hourglass!* She's still got work to do tonight.

She shakes her head and begins backing out of Gwyn's bathroom. "Anyway, sorry, I just remembered I have this thing I need to do tonight, so, yeah, I gotta go, but I had so much fun, and now I need to—"

Gwyn rushes forward and throws her arms around the babbling girl. Kim freezes. Gwyn holds her. Neither one moves.

A long, low exhale—a breath Kim has been hanging onto for years—escapes from deep within her. When she tries to inhale, it comes with an urgent, keening sound, a gasp, and a sob that catches in her throat. She fights the sound, but it only makes it worse. She can't do this here. *No, no, no.* She can't cry in front of her new friend. But she *is* crying, and now sobbing, and now wailing—uncontrollable and stupid—the kind of sobs only a little baby would make. Gwyn grips Kim tighter to keep her from collapsing into a puddle on the floor. She doesn't flinch or offer words of comfort. Gwyn doesn't say anything. She continues embracing her friend—holding her close and tight—and she doesn't let go.

# Thirteen

Kim skips down the drive to her brother's car, idling at the curb. She gets inside, beaming. "Hey, can I get a mini fridge in my room?"

Jake stares at her in horror. "Kimmy, what did you do to your hair?"

"Oh." Kim runs her fingers through her pink and blue locks. "I dyed it."

"To look like your bedroom walls?"

*Crap, he noticed, too.* "Hey, if I can have a mini-fridge, I'll let you paint my room."

"Oh wow, would you? Yeah, it's a no-go on the fridge. You spend enough time in your room. We add cold chocolate milk and fruit cups, and you'll never be seen or heard from again."

Kim leans into the passenger seat and pouts.

Jake rolls his eyes. "What? Is it because your new friend has a mini-fridge?"

"Yes! She also has three cute doggies, but I know better than to ask for one of those, you killjoy."

"Oh, I'm a killjoy now? Hey, I got an idea: Why don't you spend more time at *her* house? Lord knows you need to get out more and quit stinkin' up our place."

Kim gasps. "I'm never baking you cookies again!"

Jake laughs. "Yeah, right. You can't help yourself."

Kim sinks deeper into her seat and folds her arms across her chest.

Jake sucks in a sharp breath and holds it. Kim's noticed he does this anytime he's trying to think of what their parents might have asked if they were here. He exhales. "So Kimmy, between dying your hair, petting dogs, and eating who-knows-what from the mini-fridge, did you at least do your homework?"

"Yes."

"Hey, good job."

Jake doesn't know the half of it. Kim still has a ton of work to do tonight.

Jake takes the long way to their house, avoiding the bridge. Kim is glad for this small kindness. She hasn't seen the bridge since their parents' accident, and she doesn't want to see it. *Maybe Jake doesn't want to go near the bridge, either? He acts like everything is fine but still takes the long way to avoid it. Does he do it for me or for himself?*

When they arrive home, the house is dark. Jake unlocks the door and kicks off his shoes before stepping inside. "Listen, we gotta keep quiet. Grandma wasn't feeling great when I got home, so she went to bed early. It's nothing to freak out about. Just let her rest, okay?"

"Did you bring her tea and toast or anything?"

"Kimmy. Let Grandma rest."

The words hit Kim harder than Jake imagines. *Let Grandma rest.* Jake doesn't understand. Grandma is dead already, or somewhere between life and death, a kind of limbo-life, and now it's up to Kim to escort her soul to the Underworld for Charon to take across the river. *Charon.* She needs to get to work. She'll check on Grandma later.

When Kim reaches her room, there is a rattling sound, and it's getting louder. She opens her bedroom door, and a shimmering purple beacon of light explodes from her closet. *The hourglass!* It's rumbling, pulsating, and freaking out. Purple sand swirls and eddies, threatening to break the glass. It can't wake Grandma. Kim snatches it up and commands it to take her to her next appointment. She grabs hold of the sickle. Black robes stir and envelop her, and she vanishes.

# Fourteen

The Grim Reaper has collected eighty souls in the past fifteen minutes. She's killin' it tonight!

She's discovered souls can fit in the folds of her robes, and she doesn't always need to coax or convince them to come with her—she can scoop them up as she gallops across the land astride her trusty dappled mare. In this way, she doesn't have to dwell too long at the scenes of their deaths, which are often sad and depressing—*also gross and nauseating.* The idea of barfing into a trash bin or behind a shrub is not a good look for Death.

Two souls stand in the road ahead, staring at their house ablaze. They are detached, mere observers now, no longer invested in the loss or tragedy. Death takes them into her arms, places them in her robes where it is safe and warm, and gallops onward.

When Death arrives on the shores of the River Styx, the ferryman awaits her. His scowl does nothing to hide his annoyance as he drums his fingers against the bow.

Death dismounts and approaches. "Oh, hey! Sorry, I had school and then a whole crapload of homework and stuff, but listen, I brought you all these."

Death unfurls her robes, depositing eighty-two souls onto the beach. They look around, confusion on their faces. "Listen, guys, this is Charon. He's gonna take you on a little boat ride, doesn't that sound fun?"

The souls begin roaming in eighty-two directions, and Death must wrangle them into formation, even threatening one with her sickle to get them in line. Soon, they are filing into the boat, though they'll never all fit. Kim panics. "Um, what do we do?"

Charon snaps his gnarled fingers, and his boat replicates across the shoreline. First, there is one, and then there are forty, all with the same ancient, white-bearded man at the helm. The souls climb aboard without protest.

The Charons fix Death with an icy glare. He never talks when souls are present, but apparently his curiosity wins out. "How long did it take you?"

Death straightens her back with pride. "This group? Only fifteen minutes!"

The Charons' shoulders sag in unison, drooping further than Death thought possible. "You do realize one hundred and five people cross over every minute?"

From deep within her hooded cowl, Death's eyes widen, and a wad of bubblegum falls from her open mouth, landing in the sand at her feet. "*Every minute?*"

The Charons all nod. "You need to collect 1,575 every quarter hour. There are eighty-two here, which means you're 1,493 short."

"*What?*"

"Add to that the ten hours you wasted on school, homework, and whatever other silliness you teenagers get up to, and you've got another 63,000-soul deficit to make up. And don't even get me started on yesterday's abysmal pace."

Death huffs with indignation. This guy's got a lot of nerve criticizing her hard work. "How the heck is anybody supposed to do this job? It's frickin' impossible!"

The Charons shrug as forty boats push off into open waters. "The last person did it."

"Well, I didn't get proper training!" Death yells from the shore. "I didn't even want this stupid job!"

From the boats, eighty-two souls gasp, and the Charons glower with disappointment.

Death winces. "No, you guys are all great. I mean, I was happy to help everyone here today, it's just that, well...aw, crapola. Guys! I'm sorry!"

The boats disappear into the mist, the souls becoming eighty-two scintillating dots of light before diffusing into a warm glow within the misty fog.

"Good job, you numbskull. Well, that was a beautiful sight, at least. I wish everybody got to see it." Death is starting to think whatever is on the other side isn't anything to be afraid of— though she's still scared of almost everything else. She pulls the hourglass from her robes. "Better get back to it then."

The Reaper wonders if she can replicate herself like Charon. She doesn't think so, but she *can* stop time. For the next hour, and with every appointment, she turns the hourglass sideways and moves through a silent world, collecting souls.

Kim stops at the Central Library in Swansea, Wales, where it is already morning. She learns that Charon was telling the truth—on average, 150,000 people die every day, 6,250 every hour, and 104 each minute. *Ah, he'd said 105, the exaggerator!*

She also learns that 385,000 babies are born each day, 16,042 every hour, and 268 each minute. It's incredible that she shares a birthday with 385,000 people and that 268 were born the exact minute she came into this world. She wonders if she'll ever meet someone born the same minute as her. If there's one thing this job is teaching her—it's a vast world, after all.

Kim's parents used to say they were soulmates. They had the same birthday. They even died on the same day. The odds of it are both magic and tragic, and it hurts Kim's heart to think about it for too long. *With all the people in this world, how do soulmates find one another? Maybe it's fate or destiny, like an invisible thread that connects us with everyone we meet in this lifetime.*

Death thinks about her new best friend. Gwyn is crazy-cool and a bit scary but also super-kind—when she wants to be. Was it fate that brought them together? It started with some random note thrown in English class, and now she's told Gwyn things she hasn't told anyone.

Before Death realizes what's happened, she is standing in Gwyn's driveway. For a moment, she panics. *No, no, no, not here! Any place but here. I can't collect a soul from this house.*

The hourglass does not tug or pull her toward the front door. Death considers how she got here. She was thinking about Gwyn, and then she was here—as if the invisible thread had brought her.

The Reaper peers into the hourglass, focusing her attention on a single grain of purple sand—a soul. The air around her shifts, and she stands in a dark living room. Pre-dawn light filters through a wide bay window. A man lies on the beige carpet in the room's center. He is not moving. His soul is close, Death can feel it, though she cannot explain how. She focuses on the grain of sand again and appears upstairs in a child's bedroom. The man's soul is here, watching his two small children breathe in and out in a steady, rhythmic sleep.

"I can't go yet," he says. "They need me, and I need them."

The Reaper watches the man, her curiosity growing. Had her parents gone to her when they died? She hopes they did. But what if they didn't?

She places a comforting hand on the man's shoulder. "They know you love them."

The man shakes his head. "If I'd have known I had so little time, I would have spent more of it with them."

"I know."

The man turns to face Death, overwhelmed by anguish. "Are they going to be okay? Will they ever forgive me for leaving them? I need to know. You have to tell me."

Death doesn't know what to say. Has she forgiven her parents for leaving? Are they somewhere right now, terrified by the same fears that grip this man?

The Reaper takes the man into her arms, holding him close while he cries. She holds him for a long while and doesn't let go until she sets him inside the boat, where Charon wordlessly takes him across the river to the great mystery that lies on the other side.

# Fifteen

The Grim Reaper is dead-tired when she arrives home before sunrise. It's been a monthlong night, maybe longer, with many weeks in the saddle, galloping through a world frozen and unturning. Death is trying to catch up, but it seems she'll never meet the demands of her vocation. She tries to sleep, tossing and turning with the nagging feeling she'll never be any good at this job.

Overtired and underfed, Death rises from her bed, resolved to her cruel fate. She focuses her vision on a single grain of sand sitting in the bottom of the hourglass and soon finds herself in the presence of another soul, or close by to one, at least. She has learned an important thing about getting her job done: lost souls—ghosts, specters, apparitions—are the only things that move when time stops. Death watches with a keen eye. Any shiver on the wind tells her a soul is nearby. Most are complacent, content to move on to the Afterlife. Others—the ones who have eluded Death or have been waiting awhile—are cagier and more resistant to coming with her. It's like the longer they spend time as ghosts, the more anxious they get about leaving.

In her travels, Kim sees every type of death imaginable—in homes, on highways, in hospitals, hotel rooms, oceans, lakes, swimming pools, in desert ravines and on snowy mountaintops. Most die from natural causes—short stints and long, hard battles. Some die by another's hand—murder, war, genocide, mass shootings. Death can hardly bear it.

Suicide is something else, though. Death does not collect those. She does not know where they go, but they don't go with her. She wouldn't have noticed this except for the time when she came upon two bodies but only one soul. One of the bodies held a gun. They had shot the other—the soul Death collected—and then shot themselves. Their soul was nowhere. Kim felt a kind of relief at this—that the murderer's soul did not have to travel with the one they'd killed. But where did they go? *Do suicides go some place else?* She'll have to ask Charon about this.

Death rides on, collecting tens of thousands from every continent, and it feels like she and her mare have been on the move for months. She sleeps and eats under the same night sky, the stars unmoving in a permanent midnight that only she knows.

She wishes she had time to talk to each soul she collects, to know their stories and celebrate their lives, but there will never be enough time, even when time has stopped. With every passing second—unceasing, unending—another vivid life ceases to be. They leave families and friends forever changed by their loss. *How do we all bear it?*

Death places her sickle in her bedroom closet and sets the hourglass on its side on her nightstand. The world freezes again, and this time, without the sound of horse hooves galloping beneath her, the profound silence grips her heart and overtakes her emotions.

As she climbs into bed, tears drip onto the pillow like falling grains of sand. She doesn't know why she's crying. *There are so many things to cry about, where to start? School. Family. Friends. Darkness. Impermanence. Life. Death. Everything. It's all too hard.*

Kim rolls onto her side and a few strands of pink and blue fall across her vision. She brushes her hair from her eyes, wipes the tears, and begins laughing. *Oh my God, this hair! Love it, love it, love it.*

From her nightstand drawer, Kim pulls out a small journal. The inside cover reads *Property of Rebecca*

*Morse.* There is only one entry, entitled *Tomorrow is Another Day.*

*Each day, we get a new opportunity to be better, try harder, risk an open heart, and follow our bliss. The past is now a memory. The future remains ever uncertain. So treasure the good, learn from the bad, and know nothing is permanent. Whatever you're going through, remember that change is inevitable. Everything in your life is a season, a phase. There is no such thing as forever, and like my girl Cher says: "life is not a dress rehearsal," so enjoy each present moment. It's all you've got, sweetheart.*

Kim closes the journal and places it in the drawer. She stares at the photo of the majorette on her nightstand and her mother's face filled with joyful abandon. *This photograph is a miracle.* Kim's mother had a lot of good days—more good than bad, she'd say—but the Home Day's parade was one of her favorites ever, along with her wedding day, getting her Masters' degree, and the birth of her children. How incredible that someone was there with a camera to capture one of the great moments of her life. Kim thinks of all the people who died before the invention of photography. *How do we remember their greatest moments? How do we remember and honor all those people? One-hundred and fifty thousand leave us every day. There are more people dead than alive. Where do they all go? Agh, too many questions! Why are there always so many questions right before bed? See? That's another one!*

Kim squeezes her eyes shut, determined to quiet her racing mind. She tries to run her memory reel and a new one arrives, unbidden. Halloween, maybe when she was seven or eight. She was dressed as a giant cupcake with a cherry hat on her head, and her mother was a witch. Kim recalls holding her mother's hand as they walk through their neighborhood at night. Her mom wears black robes and a tall black hat. Kim wonders if she pushed this memory away, and now, after doing what's she's been doing each night, the memory feels safe enough to reveal itself again. She smiles at this idea, replaying this Halloween reel over and over until a flash of their arrival home comes into her mind's eye. Her father awaits them in a Frankenstein's Monster mask, and he chases them around the living room, giving out big bear hugs as he catches Kim and her mother. They fall on the couch, laughing.

Kim smiles so hard she almost cries. Are there more memories to unlock? How much has she hidden away from herself? She wishes she could see their faces, hear their laughter, but the deep love and affection in this memory is priceless to her and worth remembering, even if it's bittersweet. She drifts off to sleep, feeling closer to her parents than she's felt in a long while.

There is a moment when she stirs, but she's too tired to open her eyes. A presence like a gentle breeze crosses her face, brushing her hair from her eyes in a soothing caress.

Kim doesn't know how long she's out, but when she awakens, the sunrise is in the same spot as when she went to bed.

High school. Day three. New hair. New best friend. *You got this!*

Kim tips the hourglass upright. Time re-starts and the sudden noise and brightness descend upon her, overwhelming her senses. It's surreal. *Birds chirping! Cars driving on pavement! Life is alive and amazing!*

Kim stumbles into the bathroom, sees herself in the mirror, and screams.

# Sixteen

The Grim Reaper stares at her reflection. Her skin is pasty and pale, like some scary goth girl. *Definite vitamin D deficiency here.* Her pink and blue hair has grown out, showing two inches of dull brown roots. Her posture is terrible with shoulders slumped and back bent from weeks *(or was it months?)* in the saddle. She looks down. *Bow-legged! Nooo!*

Kim tries to straighten her back, and her spine cracks one vertebra at a time. She looks in the mirror again, scrutinizing the changes. *Sooo ooold!*

She must be an inch taller, maybe two inches. *How?* Also, her complexion is clearer, and her boobs are maybe bigger. *Like, by a smidge. Hey, gotta take the good with the bad here.*

After the initial shock wears off, she can't help but wonder if this is all a good thing. It's obvious she can't go to school like this, but she doesn't *totally hate* her new looks. Sure, she needs some color in her cheeks and a trip to a chiropractor, but overall, she's more grown-up looking, more refined, her face less babyish, leaner, and...*wiser. Maybe? Whoa, are those cheekbones? That's bonkers.*

Kim grabs the scythe from her closet. The black robes rise and swirl around her, and a moment later, she stands on the shoreline of the River Styx. She points an accusatory bony finger at the ferryman. "This is the thanks I get?"

Charon arches a brow, perplexed, but it doesn't slow Kim's tirade. "I brought you, what, 100,000 souls last night, maybe more, I was too exhausted to keep track, and this is what I get for all my hard work!"

The Reaper drops her scythe, and the robes swirl away. She stands before the ferryman in her pink footsie pajamas.

Charon makes a face like someone left an open tuna can on the counter overnight. "What the blazes did you do to your hair?"

"Not my hair! I mean my gaunt face and bent back, and my friggin' bowlegs!"

Charon regards Kim, taking a long appraising look. "I'm sorry, I can't get past the hair."

"Dammit, Charon! Forget the hair for a minute. Look at me."

"I'm looking."

"Don't you see? *I'm old.*"

Charon's face goes blank, then splutters and breaks into a gap-toothed grin. A low, wheezy rasp erupts from his open mouth, and Kim realizes he's laughing, cackling even. She wants to get angrier, but she catches herself. Kim is yelling at a man who could pass for one-hundred-twenty, and she's upset because she looks fifteen-and-a-half when she's only fifteen.

Kim starts laughing, too. Charon doubles over in his boat. Tears stream down his cheeks, and his laughter turns into a coughing fit. He looks like he might pass out.

Kim stops laughing. "Hey, you okay?"

Charon waves a hand. "Fine. I'm fine." His coughing settles, and he bends over, placing his hands on his knees to steady himself, breathing hard. "My, you're a funny one."

Kim doesn't think she's all that funny. She's sad and mad and anxious and depressed all at the same time. None of that sounds the least bit funny.

She asks herself what she's so upset about, and the answer makes her even sadder and madder. She's angry she'll never pass for twelve again. Not now, not ever. She's growing up, and it's all happening too fast. *I don't look like their little girl anymore. How will they know it's me? What if they don't recognize me? What if we forget each other? We can't forget each other!*

Kim lets out a long, dramatic sigh and doesn't care who hears. "I need to see my mom and dad. I'm done collecting souls until you bring them to me. I can't do this anymore."

"You know that isn't how this works."

"I don't care."

Charon rubs his forehead in consternation. "There's something I must tell you."

Kim stares hard at the ancient man. She wonders if he's been leading her on about seeing her parents again so he could coax her into doing this whole "Grim Reaper" thing. If he's been lying to her, she'll kill him. She's pretty sure she can do that now. She's Death.

"You've heard of the Four Horsemen?" Charon asks, his voice hesitant.

"Like, 'of the Apocalypse'? End times and all that. Yeah, sure."

"So, you know Death is one of them? Some would argue their de facto leader."

"Uh-huh, got it. I'm one of the Four Horsemen of the Apocalypse. Get to the point, Charon, I'm kinda runnin' late for school."

"The others. They're aware you've fallen behind, and...they want a word with you."

Kim scoffs. "What are they gonna do, write me up?" The ferryman shakes his head, and his grave look sends an involuntary shiver through Kim's body. "Well, what do they want?"

Charon's eyes go milky, and his voice quavers. "The end of the world."

# Seventeen

Jake strolls downstairs and stops short when he finds his sister eating cereal at the kitchen counter. She's dressed in a charcoal hoodie and dark denim jeans with her backpack over her shoulder. "Whoa, somebody's ready for school."

The Grim Reaper eats her cereal.

"You seem," Jake leans in for closer inspection, "taller."

The Grim Reaper rinses her bowl and spoon.

"And moodier. Did you catch what Grandma's got? You look kinda pasty."

The Grim Reaper dries her hands on a dish towel. "I'm fine."

"Ooh-kay. Did you check on Grandma before you came downstairs?"

"Yes, when I got up. Did you?"

"Yeah, Miss Sunshine, I just came from there. She says she's tired is all." Jake opens the fridge and pulls out an orange juice container and a loaf of bread. "Gonna bring her some juice and toast."

"Don't you think we should call her doctor or one of the neighbors? No offense to Grandma, but she looks pretty crappy, Jake. And she smells like a dead body."

"How would you know what a dead body smells like? And don't be such an alarmist. She's old and needs rest, Kimmy. And *no stress*. She'll be fine. Quit worrying so much."

*Worried? Who's worried? I just found out my new co-workers want to destroy humanity, and my grandma is a zombie. What do I have to worry about?!* Death wants to erupt at her brother, but she keeps her outburst on the inside. Instead, she snatches the bread from him. "I'll take care of it."

Jake eyes her while pouring the juice. "Thanks, you're a big help."

The Grim Reaper pops two pieces of bread into the toaster and pulls the butter and jam from the fridge. "Yep. That's me. Miss Helpful."

Jake heads upstairs with grandma's meager breakfast. "We're leavin' in five, cool?"

Kim drums her fingers on the counter, preoccupied with how she will deal with Martin, Luki, and Peggy—

better known as the Horsemen of Pestilence, War, and Famine.

"Uh-huh. I'll be ready."

# Eighteen

**D**eath wears her mother's raspberry beret to school to hide her brown roots. She ducks her head inside her locker when she sees Taylor Mead coming down the hall with her entourage.

Kim startles at a sudden *BANG!* against her locker's open metal door. She peers around and breathes with relief. It's Gwyn with her midnight ruby hair, black and gray striped button-down shirt, rhinestone skull belt buckle, ripped black jeans, and black platform boots. She's grinning. "Hey, what's with the French debutante look? You're not feelin' self-conscious about your hair, are you?" She motions to grab the beret, and Kim swats her hand.

Gwyn yanks her hand away and looks offended.

"Sorry," Kim says, her cheeks reddening. "I need to wear this, okay?"

Gwyn blows air from puffed cheeks. "Um, okay, dude. But those striped locks are super-cute. Don't hide 'em all day, *annwyl*."

Kim doesn't want Gwyn to see her brown roots. It's too ridiculous to explain how they grew out in one night. "Wait, what did you call me?"

"*Annwyl*? Means 'darling' in Welsh."

"You speak Welsh?"

Gwyn clicks her black nails against Kim's locker. "Yep."

"I've been to Swansea," Kim says without thinking. "They've got a cool library."

"When were you in Wales?"

Kim's cheeks turn a deeper shade of red. "Oh, um, it was a long time ago."

Gwyn narrows her eyes, looking from the beret down to Kim's baby blue and white saddle shoes. "Hey, did you get taller?"

Kim slouches. "I mean, maybe?"

Gwyn's eyes go wide. "You did! You, like, grew two inches overnight! What the eff, girl?"

Kim breaks into nervous laughter. "Heh, I dunno! I just, like, grew, I guess."

Gwyn scrutinizes Kim. "You're an enigma, Kim Morse. I gotta keep an eye on you."

Kim's nervous laughter ceases. "Hey, you said my name." The words fly from her mouth before she can stop them.

"What?" Gwyn looks perplexed.

"Oh, never mind. I mean—I wasn't sure you even knew my name. You always call me babe or girl or *annwyl*."

Gwyn places her hands on her hips. "I know your name, dude. In fact, I like saying it."

Kim raises an eyebrow. "Erm. When have you ever said it?"

Gwyn leans into Kim until their noses almost touch. "When I'm alone. In bed." She closes her eyes and whispers. "Kiiimmm Mooorsssse."

"Ew!" Kim shoves Gwyn, and they both burst into uncontrollable fits of laughter. Kim isn't sure why she said *ew*. She keeps laughing but she's also replaying the *ew* and the shove in her mind over and over until it becomes a confusing, jumbled feeling that she doesn't know where to put. Does Gwyn *like her* like her? And does Kim like Gwyn that way? *Whoa, maybe?*

As their laughter dies down, Gwyn fixes Kim with a somber expression. "No, seriously, I think it's a cool last name. Morse. Like, '*Pallida Mors aequo pulsat pede pauperum tabernas regumque turres,*' or something like that."

Kim scrunches her nose. "Is that Welsh again?"

"It's Latin. My grandfather was a professor of classic literature. Taught me a bunch of famous quotes before he died."

"Sorry about your grandpa."

"Yeah, no worries. He got kinda weird at the end. I was the only one who could understand him, always going back-and-forth from English to Welsh to Latin every third sentence. I'd have to translate for my mom and the nurses."

"Sorry."

Gwyn levels her gaze. "What did I tell you about apologizing all the time?"

Kim rolls her eyes. "Fine, then I'm not sorry. But what did you say? Like, what does it mean?"

"Pretty sure it's Horace, but it might be Seneca or some other dead Roman. The quote is 'Pale Death, with impartial step, kicks at the huts of paupers and the palaces of kings.' You get it?"

"Uh-huh. Everybody dies. But which word was my name?" Kim gets light-headed and clenches the locker door to hold herself upright. She thinks she knows the answer to her question but doesn't want to know.

*"Pallida Mors?"* Gwyn asks, eyes saucer-like for effect. "Pale. Death."

In English class, Mrs. Bell asks the students if they're at all envious of Dorian Gray. Most students agree it would be cool to be like Dorian—to never grow old. To be immortal. To have your evil deeds and vain worries appear on the face of your portrait rather than your own. Taylor Mead raises her hand to bring up the benefits of never having wrinkles or cellulite. Mrs. Bell fixes her with a withering look but admits most students agree with Taylor. Mrs. Bell says it's like that every year but tells the class that the tone changes with people her age. Her peers rarely want to be like Dorian.

Kim raises her hand, and Mrs. Bell nods her way.

"I think I know why," Kim says, quieting her voice.

Mrs. Bell looks intrigued. "Speak up, Miss Morse, I want to hear this."

"When you're young, like a toddler or something, and you wander out into the world and see a flower, you can't help but pick it. It's so beautiful and sweet. You take it home and put it in water and a few days later, it dies. That's maybe our first understanding of death. But it doesn't end there. It never ends. I think it's all death from there on out. Or, *loss* might be a better word. We're dealing with loss all the time. People die every day, and they leave us here to grieve their passing. And then we grow old and die and are hopefully reunited with the ones who went before us. I think someone like Dorian, if he doesn't get older, he feels disconnected from every living thing. I think he must be super-lonely because he can't appreciate the fleeting beauty of life. And worse, he's gotta stand by and watch as everyone he's ever cared for dies all around him. He's going to lose everyone he loves. The one way I'd want to live forever is if everyone gets to live forever with me. But I think the only way to have that is to die."

"Die?" Mrs. Bell asks, arching a brow.

Kim squirms in her seat then decides, if she's come this far, why not keep talking and officially out herself as a morbid freak? "I just think, if there's a place we all go, like heaven or wherever, then we'll get to be there together. So, it's better to die than live forever among strangers."

Mrs. Bell furrows her brow. "That's an interesting thought, albeit a bit morose, Miss Morse."

"Well, I just learned my last name means Death."

The class snickers and Kim exchanges a knowing glance with Gwyn.

"Well, you've made some compelling points," Mrs. Bell says. "We'll keep reading the book and see if anyone else comes around to your way of seeing it. Of course, I'm not advocating for anyone taking their life or anything. That's not what you're saying, are you, Miss Morse?"

"Oh, no, no. I'm not saying that at all."

Mrs. Bell purses her lips and nods. "Okay, good."

The bell rings, and as the students rush out of the room, Mrs. Bell asks Kim to stay behind for a moment. Gwyn waits at the door, trying not to look like she's spying on the conversation, but she is.

"Do you read much?" Mrs. Bell asks.

"I guess. I like libraries and my dad used to read a lot. He'd share stories with me and stuff."

"You ever think about becoming a writer?"

"Um. Not really."

"I always say the best writing starts with a fresh perspective, a way of seeing the world a tad askew from the rest of us. You've got that askew-ness about you."

"Um, okay. Are you saying I'm weird?"

"Mm-hmm. But in a good way." Mrs. Bell pulls a pamphlet from her desk drawer. "I teach a creative writing class in the evenings at the community college. There's space if you're interested."

Kim takes the flyer. "Okay, but my brother would have to drive me, and he's always super busy in the evenings."

"Well, you ask him. And tell him to come see me if he has any questions."

"Okay. Thanks, Mrs. Bell."

"Sure, kid. Now don't let me keep you from your next class."

Kim grins. "Okay."

Mrs. Bell's eyelids fall to half-mast. "And stop saying okay so damn much."

"Okay." Kim rushes out the door and locks arms with Gwyn as they scurry down the hall, giggling.

# TWenty

Kim chews on the stale, easy-cheesy pepperoni pizza bites she packed for lunch. She's only eating them to reward herself with the packet of milk chocolate gems afterward—the magenta ones are her favorites. "Can this day go any slower?" She's whining again.

"Flyin' by for me," Gwyn replies through a mouthful of hummus-veggie sandwich on toasted seed bread. Kim's discovered Gwyn is a vegan, and she thinks the whole concept sounds insane.

Kim glances from her bento box tray of kids' munchies to Gwyn's grown-up sandwich and sighs. "Well, I can't wait to leave here. I have a ton of work."

"You should quit that babysitting job," Gwyn says. "Come work with me."

"You have a job?"

"Yeah, at Happy Valley Barn two days a week. Horse stables. It's super-chill there."

"Oh, I love horses," Kim replies, thinking of Snowball. She's decided to name Death's horse Snowball because of the mare's ice-cold nose. She hasn't told anyone else the name, but Snowball seems to like it because her ears perk whenever Death whispers it into her twitching ear during their extended night-time rides together. Maybe she should tell Charon the name? That way, whoever takes over her job next knows their mare is called Snowball, and that—

"Hey!" Gwyn shoves Kim's arm. "Are you even listening?"

Kim jolts with alarm. "Sorry."

Gwyn narrows her eyes. "What. Did. I—"

"Okay, okay!" Kim laughs. "I'm not sorry. But tell me what you were saying. I got distracted thinking about horses."

Gwyn huffs. "Fine. I was saying we should go riding together."

Kim thinks about her sore buttocks and bowlegs and wonders if riding a horse during the day could make her posture and soreness any worse at this point. "Yeah, sure. Let's go riding."

"Cool. Ride or die, babe." Gwyn takes a bite of her grown-up sandwich. Kim gazes across the street and notices a man in quilted lifida-style armor and a sulke chainmail shirt. She recalls seeing a photograph of a man in a similar outfit in a book her father had read on the history of Africa.

The man stands on the corner, looking like a cosplayer from 15th Century northern Nigeria. Kim continues watching and gets creeped out by the man's determined stance and penetrating gaze. She peers closer. The man's stare turns venomous as he mouths the words, *Found you.*

"Hey," Kim snatches Gwyn's arm and shakes it. "You see that creepy guy over there?"

Gwyn looks up. "Who?"

"Across the street. He's like an African warrior guy."

Gwyn looks at Kim and back to where the man is standing. "There's nobody over there, Kim."

Kim doesn't want to point at him, but she does anyway. "He's right there."

Gwyn's tone shifts to one of concern. "Are you seeing ghosts or something?"

The man's face is filthy with sweat and grime, yet he's grinning now. It's a wicked smile that shows off his chipped and missing teeth but doesn't reach his dead eyes. Kim feels the raw hatred radiating from the man, and it chills her. "You don't see that guy? You swear it?"

"Are you having, like, a *sixth sense* moment here? Or is this your idea of a weird joke?" Gwyn takes Kim's face in her hands. "Babe, hey. There's nobody there."

Kim pulls her face away from Gwyn's touch and looks across the street. Empty. The man is gone. Relief washes over Kim, and she starts giggling to keep from crying. "I had you going."

"No, you didn't." Gwyn furrows her brow. "You're strange."

"But it's the good kind of strange, right?"

"Yeah, not always."

Kim glances again to confirm no one is across the street. Was it a ghost? Her job is to look for them, but what if they can find her, too? And did he say *found you* or were Kim's eyes playing tricks on her? Could it have been Luki? Charon told her about Luki this morning—the Horseman of War. The guy *was* wearing armor. Kim tries to shake off the terror, decides she's being paranoid, and heads to her next class.

The Grim Reaper's third day at school continues to drag. Her mind keeps drifting to the Horsemen of the Apocalypse. She's unable to shake the feeling of dread. How will she deal with them? The seconds tick by in perpetual slow motion, and there's an ache in the pit of her stomach that makes her feel like a gut-shot gunslinger waiting to die. When the last bell rings, she races to Jake's car, but he isn't there. She remains a while until Danny and Brian stroll over.

"Where is he?"

Brian drops his backpack by the car door. "Still with Mrs. Margaret, I guess."

The name Margaret flashes red neon in Kim's mind as she recalls the name of the third Horseman. Peggy is a nickname for Margaret. Kim's paranoia sets in all over again. "Who's Mrs. Margaret? Does anybody call her Peggy?"

Brian laughs. "Peggy? What?"

Danny shoots Kim a look like she's the dumbest person on the planet. "Mrs. Margaret is our school principal, Dippy."

Kim wants to kick him. It's her third day at this school. How's she supposed to know the name of the principal? *Okay, fine. So she's not the Horsewoman of Famine.*

"Why is Jake talking to her? Is he in trouble?"

Brian looks confused. He always looks confused. "Nah, I think she's talking to him about colleges or something."

*College.* Kim's paranoia grows. She hadn't considered that Jake might leave for college after graduation. What will happen when Grandma passes and Jake goes to university on the other side of the country? *There'll be no one left!*

Kim turns and speed-walks toward home. She needs her scythe, the hourglass, and her mighty steed.

"Hey, where ya goin'?" Brian asks.

"Yeah, he'll be here in a minute," Danny calls.

Kim continues walking as if on a mission. She puts in her earbuds and plays her favorite song on repeat while she walks. She needs to block out the world until she can figure out what to do next.

She needs to talk to Charon.

# Twenty-One

Kim arrives home and races upstairs. She cracks open Grandma's bedroom door to find her still in bed. "Hey, how ya feeling?"

Grandma struggles to roll over. When she does, her face is even pastier than Kim's complexion. Her cracked lips break into a forced smile. "Oh, hey, Kimmy girl. I'm okay, sweetie. Just a little cold, is all."

Kim steps into the room and tucks the knitted quilt closer around her grandmother's body. "Need anything?"

"I made myself some tea earlier." Grandma's voice sounds like a diesel truck rolling down an unpaved road.

Kim wants to lean in and smother her grandmother with hugs and kisses, to be held in her arms the way she used to, but the smell in the room makes her want to hurl, so she backs up toward the doorframe. "Well, you're not coughing as much. That's good, right?"

"Sure, hon."

"Okay, I'll let you rest. Love you, Grandma."

"Love you too, Kimmy."

She eases the door shut while swallowing back tears. She takes a deep breath of stale, but not nauseating, hallway air. In her room, she retrieves the scythe and hourglass from her closet.

"God help me."

The room spins, and soon, she stands at the water's edge.

The ferryman eyes the Grim Reaper as if he's been waiting for her all day. He drums his fingers against the bow. "Anything for me?" Charon asks, and even Kim picks up on his peevish tone.

"Not now, Charon. First, you need to tell me how to stop the horsemen, save my grandma, and quit this job. And I want to see my parents."

Charon pulls at his beard again and makes a face like he's bitten into a sour apple and found half a worm in it. "I don't know how to do any of that."

"Well, who does?"

Charon's eyes alight as if he's had a sudden revelation. "Go see Syn!"

Kim scrunches her nose. "Who's that? I thought you were gonna say go see Moses or St. Peter or even Hades."

Charon stiffens, and his lips go white as they press together. "Hades is a donkey's arse! I'd never send you to him. Syn is many things—wicked yet benevolent, sneaky but kind—and committed to justice above all else. You'll never know what you'll get with her. She's a fate spirit, a Disir, who became a goddess. You like fate and goddesses, don't you?"

Kim's eyelids fall to half-mast. "Eh, not really."

"Be that as it may, she is the defender and gatekeeper at the door to the Otherworld. Go talk to her."

"Um, okay. I thought this was the gateway?"

"There are many entry points," Charon says with a spark in his gray eyes. "You should know that by now."

"So, how do I find her?"

Charon shrugs. "You're Death. With that hourglass, you can locate just about anybody."

Death stares into her hourglass, willing it to take her to see the infamous Syn, fate spirit and gatekeeper to the Otherworld. "Okay. Concentrate."

The cavern and underground river melt away as shimmering light fills the Reaper's vision. When her eyes refocus, she stands in front of Gwyn's house. She looks to the upstairs window and finds Gwyn doing homework at her desk. Kim wishes she could be with

Gwyn right now—wishes she didn't have to be Death in this black robe and heavy cowl. She wishes for a lot of things.

She's too distracted to find Syn right now. Maybe she should knock on Gwyn's door, spend some time with her new best friend, pet her three floppy-eared hounds, eat chocolate pudding from the mini-fridge, and forget about stopping the end of the world. Maybe she should tell Gwyn everything? Would Gwyn think she was insane?

*Yes. Yes, she would.*

Death regards her hourglass with a rueful gaze. "Lotta help you are." The hourglass vibrates in her hand. "I can't tell if that means you're irritated or afraid."

The hourglass vibrates harder, as if trying to shake itself from Death's skeletal grip. The streetlights blink out, and a heavy fog fills the night air.

"Ah, zere you are."

Death spins on her heel. Three figures astride horses emerge from the gloom at the end of the lane.

The first man rides a sickly white stallion. Its eyes are empty pools of milk, and a pale green foam sits at the edges of its mouth. The white-haired rider—with his hard, ice-blue eyes—wears pale green surgeon's scrubs. He carries a bow on his back and a quiver of arrows at his side. A green mist wafts up from his quiver of arrows.

*Martin, Horseman of Pestilence.*

The second rider rips from the fog, wearing quilted armor and brandishing a large sword. He gallops full speed on a blood-soaked bay stallion. The hoofbeats sound like rapid cannon fire as they thunder past Kim. The armored man yanks the reins, sending the horse onto its hind legs in a violent turn. They halt, and Death feels the hot breath of the angry steed on her shoulder.

*Luki, Horseman of War.*

The third rider is wire-thin, built like a marionette come to life, on an emaciated black horse. She strolls in like she has all the time in the world. Her hair falls in stringy black ringlets in front of her face, and she carries a brass balancing scale in one hand. The woman's left leg is missing at the knee, replaced by an antique wooden prosthesis. *Whoa, that cannot be the reason they call her...*

*Peggy, Horsewoman of Famine.*

But it is.

The Reaper realizes too late that they've surrounded her—Martin in front, Luki behind, and Peggy at her side. There's nowhere to run.

Death stows the hourglass and lifts her scythe in a defensive stance.

A wry chuckle creeps from Martin's thin lips. The haughty sound of it pisses Kim off.

"What do you want?" she asks from within her heavy black cowl.

"Now, now," Martin says, his voice like grimy oil leaking from a rusted can. "Iz zat any vay to greet old friends?"

"She's a *foni!*" Luki yells, blood vessels popping behind his yellowed eyes. "What did you do with the Reaper, you filthy impostor?"

Death steps back, keeping the scythe ready in case one of them pounces.

"Does she...know...about the prophecy?" Peggy's voice is a measured hiss dripping with contempt. "Tell her, Martin."

The Horseman of Pestilence takes a moment to blow a stream of snot from his nose. It lands on the ground near Death's feet. "Ze boatman haz already told her, no doubt."

"He didn't tell me anything about a prophecy," Kim replies from within her cowl. *Or did he?* She isn't sure. She was tired. And hungry.

"Oh, no?" Martin asks. "Vell, zen. Give us ze hourglaz and ve'll tell you all about ze meaning of ze death child."

Death child? Was that her? And they want the hourglass? The Reaper reaches into her robes. Martin's eyes alight in anticipation. The purple translucence glows brighter as it emerges. Luki kicks his steed into a gallop, hoping to snatch the hourglass away, but before he can grab it, the Reaper casually tips it sideways.

The world stops, and the Horsemen all freeze.

Kim steps closer to them and stares into each of the Horsemen's frozen faces. "You! Stupid! Jerks!"

She reaches into her robes to retrieve a miniature marble horse. Keeping the hourglass turned sideways, she throws the figurine onto the lawn in front of Gwyn's house, yelling, "Vita mutator, non tollitur!"

A spray of cold erupts into the air, leaving a thin layer of hoarfrost on everything. Snowball emerges from the mist, and without hesitating, Kim leaps and floats onto the pale mare's back.

Keeping the hourglass turned sideways, the horse and rider gallop into the hazy night. Kim stares at the purple grains, focusing on a small cluster of sand floating in mid-air. As she gazes closer, she and her mighty steed blink out of sight.

# Twenty-Two

Death rides her pale horse on an empty mountain road at night. Her mind ping-pongs between how she will find Syn the gatekeeper, how to keep the horsemen from hunting her down, and if she needs to keep time stopped for the foreseeable future. *Well, obviously, to avoid those nutjobs.*

Death thinks she's already figured out why they want the hourglass. What happens if it breaks and all the sand leaks out? The living above and the dead below are all thrown together on the ground amongst so much shattered glass. It sure sounds like the set-up for the end of the world.

Snowball stops cold in the middle of the road and lets out a soft whinny. Kim looks around and listens for the wind through the pines, but the air is still.

"What is it, girl?"

Snowball shakes her head and clomps a single hoof on the asphalt repeatedly until Kim notices the twisted, broken guardrail at the road's edge. *Oh, crapola.* She dismounts and approaches to peer over the ledge.

At the bottom of the incline sits a battered yellow school bus on its side.

"Oh, no. No, no, no." The Reaper doesn't want to collect souls right now, not tonight, but there might be children down there, lost and scared. Death sighs with resignation. "Good girl," she mutters to the horse, patting the mare's neck with a skeletal hand. Snowball snorts in reply. Death sets the hourglass on its side at the edge of the mountain road and places a few rocks around it to keep it from rolling away.

She stands at the bent guardrail, gripping her scythe for moral support. How is she going to get down there? She does not like heights.

The Reaper holds her breath and leaps off the ledge, her black robes billowing as she floats to the scene of the accident. *Oh, this isn't so bad.*

When she reaches the bottom, she finds two dozen souls sitting in the bus, which explains the cluster of sand particles in the hourglass she was focusing on earlier. A large, heavy marching drum, cracked from the impact, blocks the bus's door from opening. Kim suddenly recalls one of her father's infamous dad jokes.

*"What's the perfect gift? A broken drum. It can't be beat."*

*Ha-ha, Dad.* She almost giggles, almost cries, at this unlocked memory of her father's bad jokes. Then she stills as she notices the souls all looking her way.

Realization hits Kim: this is a marching band. Their story comes to her as if she's known it all along. They played at a stadium event in the next county—the largest venue they'd ever performed in. For many of these kids, it was the highlight of their time at high school. They played together with such passion, synchronized from the first downbeat, and now, they've all died together in the same split-second. *"Tight band."*

*Too soon, Dad.*

The marching band watches the black-robed figure through a spider-cracked windshield. They don't know where to go or how to get out of the bus. Death is grateful they're not panicking. Not yet, anyway. It's funny how complacent souls are once they free themselves from their bodies. Kim expected they would freak out anytime they saw her, but they don't. *I mean, ghosts and ghouls can be buttheads, and for a lot of souls, there's remorse for those they're leaving behind, but for most, it's like all the anxiety and sadness disappear. They're ready.*

Kim's mother once told her that if she was feeling sad, she was overthinking the past. And, if Kim was anxious, she was overthinking the future. There is only peace and contentment in the present moment. Souls have become unbound by time—they are all that still move whenever Death stops the clock, so there's nothing for them to get emotional over. They simply exist.

Sometimes, people who seem super-happy are trying to stay positive because they don't want anyone to see how sad they are—like Kim. The rainbows, unicorns, and mermaids, the bright colors, cookies, and cupcakes—she's extra-cheery, so she doesn't have to think about the earth-shattering sadness of not having her parents around to watch her grow, to look after her, to celebrate every beautiful moment this life brings and even the simple mundane moments spent sitting around the breakfast table, no one talking, everyone doing their thing, but...*together*.

The Reaper takes her scythe and slams it into the bus. She digs the blade into the metal side with an ear-splitting scrape and rips a gaping hole large enough for everyone to climb out.

The band pulls themselves from the wreckage one by one until the last kid—a grinning, round-faced boy with shaggy blonde hair, starts handing all the instruments to his bandmates.

Death looks around, perplexed. "What are you guys doing?"

A girl holding a trombone asks. "Where's the football field?"

"Field? There's no..." A sudden bolt of inspiration shuts Death's mouth mid-sentence. The Reaper takes her scythe, spins it over her head, and begins marching. "With me!" she calls, her voice echoing through the moonlit chasm.

The marching band falls into formation behind their scythe-wielding majorette. Death high steps into the air, floating up, rising higher toward the road, toward her mare, who looks down at them with alert, pale-blue eyes.

The marching band follows, stepping into the air. The band plays a traditional John Philip Sousa song, but the blonde boy who passed the instruments stops them.

"Hey! Wait! Hang on!"

The band pauses their tune, and Death turns to see what mischief this kid is trying to pull. She recalls how much guiding souls resembles herding cats, so she needs to keep them moving in a constant direction toward the ferryman. It's either that or stuff them into the many pockets in her robes, but she can't help but feel this group needs to make this journey on their terms—together, as a band. Like a family.

A playful grin creases the blonde boy's dimpled cheeks. He knows what's happening. He might be the only one who's figured it out already. "Listen, guys, if we're goin' out together, we're doin' it right. Play the favorite!"

The band seems to awaken as if from a dream. They look around, see the bus smashed at the bottom of the ravine, their bodies lying motionless inside. They turn to the grinning boy and nod in understanding. Their gazes return to their new majorette as they wait for her to kick off the tempo.

Death has no idea what to do. "Um, what are we playin'?"

"Pshh, I'll start it," the blonde boy says, bringing a tuba to his lips. He kicks off a low bass riff, and the drummers jump in with the backbeat.

*Bum, bum, bum, badum-bum, dum-da-bum.*

The band enters, falling into the infectious rhythm, marching in place, waiting to follow Death into the void.

Kim knows this song, and she can't help but smirk. "O-M-G! Seriously? *Another One Bites the Dust*? You're all crazy!" Her smirk turns to a toothy, skeletal grin, knowing how much her dad would enjoy the inappropriateness of this song.

The band becomes joyous, rocking, playing their hearts out, and they keep playing until Death cannot resist taking up her scythe to lead them onward.

As Death strides down the mountain road, leading the band toward the river Styx, she wonders if her passion for being in a marching band is anywhere close to these kids. *It isn't.* Marching band was her mother's passion when she was a teenager, and Kim has been wanting it for herself so she can feel closer to her, but now she's certain it won't work. That obnoxious Taylor Mead can have the lead majorette role. *Who cares?* There are other ways to stay connected to Mom and Dad. She can bake or draw. She can also write, like Mrs. Bell suggested. she'll tell stories to help herself and others through their sadness and grief. She'll tell stories that give people hope and make them cry and laugh and feel.

And, with this thought at the center of her mind—this revelation that what she thought she wanted she does not want at all—Death whispers a prayer to the heavens that lights up her heart as she leads the band into the Underworld, all playing their hearts out one last time.

They were so young, and yes, this accident is tragic, but they lived their lives with passion until the last breath...and beyond. That's a life well-lived, even if they were gone too soon. When Kim's time comes, that's how she wants to go.

# Twenty-Three

**W**hen the marching band reaches the river's edge, Death tips her hourglass for the briefest moment, so Charon can replicate his boats and take them across. As they recede into the fog, the band turns up the volume on their rendition of *Another One Bites the Dust* as if their lives depended upon it. For dead folks, it's an impressive level of commitment and enthusiasm.

Death waves goodbye as the band members transform into points of light, and the music echoes and fades in a diffused glow. Once she knows the souls are on the other side (or wherever they end up), she tips the hourglass again. Kim can't let the Horsemen find her before she's had a chance to meet with Syn and see if this fate goddess can help her.

Death stares into the hourglass, focusing her attention on finding Syn. Moments later, she is on Gwyn's front lawn again. "What the actual—"

Snowball shakes her mane and snorts.

"I was focusing, I swear!"

At least the Horsemen left during that short window when she started up time again. Kim knows they can't have gone far, but why is she here again? An eerie thought prickles at the back of her mind.

The Reaper floats to Gwyn's bedroom window to check on her and ensure the Horsemen didn't kidnap her new best friend. Death expects to catch a glimpse of Gwyn's frozen form sitting at her desk doing homework, but instead, she finds the goth girl staring out the window, her face serene, as if waiting for someone to climb through it. Kim peers closer. Gwyn's three hounds sleep at her feet. *Wait.* Kim's eyes go wide. *Gwyn's three dogs are one dog with three heads!*

The Reaper drops her scythe and the robes flutter away to reveal Kim's shocked face and colored hair with the roots grown out. She sets the hourglass upright on Gwyn's writing desk, and the world springs to life like the gears of a great machine.

The three-headed dog pops its heads up and splits into three separate hounds, who begin jumping up to greet the intruder.

Gwyn's face breaks into a wide grin. "Took you long enough." She points to the scythe at Kim's feet. "Hey, nice blade, by the way."

Kim is miffed. *Like, ultra-super-duper miffed.* Somebody's been messing with her, and she's got a hunch it's her so-called best friend. "What the heck is going on here, Gwyn? I saw your dogs—they were one three-headed dog a second ago. And is your real name, Syn?"

Gwyn smirks. "I mean, sure, some folks call me Syn. Some call me Ridwan, or Niyo, and even St. Peter, which gets super-awkward. To some people, I look like a nameless owl—also awkward. But I prefer Gwyn ap Nudd. Every culture has a gatekeeper, someone who admits entry to the afterlife." Gwyn grins with outstretched arms. "IT ME!"

"You're all of them?" Kim eyes her with suspicion.

Gwyn gives Death some side-eye in return. "Uh, yeah, Kim. Think about it. Zeus, Jupiter, Odin, Olorun, Tennin—every culture and tribe has a name for their creator. News flash—they're all basically the same guy. Gods and goddesses are expert shapeshifters. They adapt to whoever they appear in front of—they look like whoever they need to be—to align with a culture's myths and connect with their followers. Sometimes, when people see me, all they see is their favorite grandparent or loved one. Someone once thought I was

Mark Wahlberg. I guess they had a crush or something. So, yeah, we adapt and transform based on the eye of the beholder. Get it? You can't tell me you haven't noticed how different you look when traveling across continents."

Kim *had* noticed her appearance changing in subtle (and sometimes dramatic) ways wherever she travels. These mythological changes are how people recognize and accept her in each place. *It's kinda random, but it works.* "Okay, I think I get your point."

"Yeah, good job. Even the dogs get it. Sometimes, when no one's looking, they slip into their three-headed form, Cerberus, but they stay separate most of the time. They're my spectral hounds of Annwn. *Aren't you, my good boys?*" Gwyn scratches the hounds' chins in turn. "Oh, and pro-tip—never take them to Valhalla. They turn into dire wolves and go all feral. Learned that the hard way my first year."

"First year?"

"Yeah, like you. I am descended from gatekeepers. When my grandfather decided to make his transition, he bequeathed the role to me. And at some point, whenever I want to move on, the role will fall to one of my descendants."

"Wait. Are you saying this Grim Reaper job is, like, a family business?"

"Uh. Yeah, silly. I told you before, your last name means death. Seriously, that didn't tip you off? Nobody's ever explained this to you? Your parents didn't—*oooh shite!* They didn't, did they? There wasn't time. I bet they thought it would be your all-star brother. Wonder if they told him? *HA!* Wait 'til he hears this."

"We're not telling him anything! No one can know. And I need your help, Gwyn. The Horsemen of Pestilence, War, and Famine all want this hourglass. They want to break the world."

"Oh, I'm sure they do. Bully the newbie—that's always how those three roll. Well, you can outsmart them. I wouldn't worry."

Kim shakes her head, hoping to clear the muddling, foggy thoughts. "I am worried, Gwyn. And wait, hang on. *Hang on!* How did you know who I was and why didn't you say anything sooner?"

"Charon told me, obviously. We see each other a lot. I'm the one waiting across the river. The gatekeeper, get it?"

"Oh. But—"

"Yeah, he couldn't bring you to me. That's not how this works. You had to find me here in the physical world. So, I made it easier on you and talked my mom into letting me transfer schools."

"But—"

"Yeah, no, I couldn't just come out and tell you. I wish we could be more like muses and hit you over the head with a spark of inspiration, but that's not how fate spirits and gatekeepers work. You gotta find *us*. There are rules, babe. I don't make 'em, but I gotta respect 'em. Blame humanity."

Kim thinks about the avalanche of work it takes to collect souls. "But how do you do it? I mean, how do you do your job as a gatekeeper with so many souls coming through every day."

"Oh, I can stop by whenever and send, like, a couple hundred thousand through in under two hours."

"So they just wait around until you decide to show up?"

Gwyn laughs. "Pretty sure it's called Purgatory, dude. They can wait until I've got time for them."

Kim slumps onto Gwyn's bed, trying to digest and make sense of all she's heard. "So, when I hit the Grim Reaper with my majorette baton, was that—"

"Your majorette baton?" Gwyn stifles a laugh.

"Yes! Stop laughing! I'm asking was it, like, my grandfather or, like, a great uncle?"

Gwyn sits on the bed next to Kim. "Does it matter? Were you guys close?"

"I mean, Dad never took me around his side of the family. And I already live with my mom's one remaining family member, so it can't be Grandma. Death was coming for her."

"I wouldn't worry about who you hit with a baton. There's one rule I'm sure of: *What's done is done.*"

"Guess you're right. But I still need your help getting Martin, Luki, and Peggy off my back."

Gwyn snorts with derision. "Peggy. Can you believe she lets them call her that?"

"I dunno." Kim falls backward, stretching her arms across Gwyn's bed.

Gwyn lays down next to her. "Hey. We'll figure it out."

"What if they find me again and...what's the word? *Ambush* me?"

Gwyn turns on her side to face Kim, resting her head in the crook of Kim's arm. "You should find them first. *You* should ambush *them.*"

"And then what?"

"You're Death!" Gwyn boops Kim's nose with her index finger. "So listen up: you lay down the law with those goofballs. Don't let them push you around."

Death smirks and rubs her eyes. She's so tired. And scared. Too tired and scared to do any of this. "Can't somebody else—"

"EHH!" Gwyn goes off like a game-show buzzer. "No, babe. You're holding the hourglass, so that means it's your responsibility to keep humanity safe. That's the deal."

Kim bolts upright. "Keep them safe? I take them away from everything and everyone they love."

Gwyn takes Kim's face in her hands. "Oh no, my annwyl. You bring them *home.*"

Kim feels a heat in her chest. It rises into her throat, burning and tingling her cheeks and ears. The urge to kiss Gwyn almost overtakes her, but that can't be right. She's never wanted to kiss anyone. She pulls away, hoping the feeling will pass. "Okay, I need to go find them and shut this down. I don't know where to start, but will you come with me?"

Gwyn quirks a brow. "A wild hunt, you say? Count me in, broski. When do we leave?"

The Reaper grabs her scythe and the black robes swirl around her. She yawns and rubs her exposed neck vertebrae. "I'm gonna need some sleep first."

"Uh, you don't have to leave. You can stay here if you want. I mean, whatever you wanna do. It's cool."

Death begins climbing out the window. "No, I need my own bed, but thanks anyway."

"Sure, sure. Get some rest. First thing tomorrow, we ditch school and go horsemen hunting."

*Ditch school?* "Wait, what?" The Reaper waves her hands as if trying to erase the idea. She loses her balance and tips backward.

Gwyn snatches a skeletal wrist to keep Death from falling out the window. She fixes the Reaper with a withering gaze. "Kim Morse, are you seriously gonna tell me *saving humanity* isn't a good enough excuse to ditch *one day* of high school?"

Death groans and pulls her wrist from Gwyn's grasp. "Ugh, you're turning me into such a rule-breaker."

Gwyn smirks. "You love me, admit it."

The Reaper straightens her cowl. "See you tomorrow morning, weirdo."

Death floats down from the second-story window, coming to rest on the back of her pale horse grazing on the lawn.

She glances up to find Gwyn watching from her bedroom window. As horse and rider trot down the wet road and disappear into the foggy night, Kim swears she hears Gwyn whisper, "Sweet dreams, space cowboy."

# Twenty-Four

**K**im studies her house from the neighbor's backyard. It doesn't look like the horsemen are there waiting to pounce, but she can't be too careful. She decides to tip the hourglass sideways and approach, hoping that, with time stopped, she can sneak up on *them* if they're around.

By the time she reaches the kitchen, she's sure they aren't here. She isn't tired—more like exhausted, but far too amped-up and stressed-out to sleep. In the kitchen, as if on autopilot, she pulls the ingredients for her mother's famous double-chocolate cupcakes with salted caramel frosting. She sets everything on the counter and brews a small pot of coffee—her mother's secret ingredient for the batter. Thanks to Grandma, there is always coffee in the house.

While the cupcakes bake, Kim heads upstairs to check on her grandmother. She panics when she sees how still and silent Grandma is, but then remembers she stopped time and shouldn't expect her grandmother to be breathing.

Kim kneels at the bedside to run her fingers through Grandma's thinning white hair. Kim's nose scrunches. The woman doesn't smell right. She needs to take her to Charon soon, but she hates the idea of it. Jake in college, Grandma gone, no one to look after her, and on her own—it's all too much. *Nope, nope. Gotta check on the cupcakes.*

As Kim passes Jake's room, she cracks open his door. He's not there. *Where could he have gone? Does Jake have a girlfriend? He better not get her pregnant!*

She considers the idea of Jake skipping college because he needs to get a job and support a new family. She thinks about him staying home to look after her and missing out on college. Jake *needs* to go to college, even if it means she'll have no one.

Kim takes the cupcakes from the oven, sets them on the counter, and curls up in her father's lounge chair while they cool. She puts in her earbuds and plays her favorite song on repeat, the one she and her mother would always dance to while belting out all the words. She dozes off and doesn't know how long she is asleep, but when she feels that familiar light breeze like invisible fingers brushing through her hair, she bolts upright.

Kim squints, rubs her eyes, trying to comprehend what she's seeing. "Daddy?"

# Twenty-Five

Charlie Morse's routine has grown past the point of monotony. Every day, he sits at his desk and stares out the window, wondering why he spends so much time working. It's as if he's responding to the same work email again and again, yet for some inexplicable reason, the hours fly by, and nothing gets done. It's another morning, then nighttime again, and he is finding less and less time for his wife and two children. He doesn't remember what he ate for lunch or if he's eaten anything in recent memory.

Something about that doesn't make sense to Charlie. All he knows is that he needs to provide for his family, keep them safe, so he works. Late at night, he wanders upstairs to check on his children. He sits at the edge of his daughter's bed and strokes her hair. Kimmy is his angel, such a sweet girl. And his son, Jake, what a bright young man he's becoming. Charlie loves his kids. He'd do anything for them.

Charlie floats to his bedroom and finds his mother-in-law sleeping there. He needs to talk to Rebecca about how long she plans to have her mother visiting. Charlie likes Sadie, but the cigarette smoke is a bit much, and he doesn't understand why Becca offered their bedroom. He looks for his wife in the guest bedroom and living room sofa but can't find her. He can never seem to find her anymore. Charlie loves Rebecca. They're soulmates. That's what they always say, but she seems so distant these past few months—or has it been years? Charlie can't tell anymore.

He struggles to recall the last time he saw Becca. He can't tell for sure, but he feels like she's there anytime Kimmy bakes cookies or cupcakes. It's like the scent of it calls Becca out from wherever she's hiding, but he still can't see her, as if there is a veil between them, paper thin, but enough to block his view.

Something is worrying Charlie, and he can't put a name to it. The past few days, things have felt different with his children. Jake's seldom in his room anymore, and Kimmy—when he watches her sleep, it feels like she has the weight of the world on her shoulders.

He smells cupcakes. Becca is close, but Charlie can't see her. He does see Kimmy dozing in his favorite lounge chair. He strokes her hair, and for the first time in many, many nights, his daughter awakens.

Kim pulls the headphones from her ears and starts crying. Why is she so upset? Or is she happy to see him? He can't tell—it's all so confusing.

Charlie tells Kim he can't find her mom. Kim tells him something, but it sounds so outlandish and illogical that he grows distressed. Why would she tell him he and Becca are dead? It makes no sense. That's no way for his sweet little girl to talk. But she's so happy to see him. She's crying so hard, hugging him even harder—could she be telling the truth?

"You're the ghost," his daughter tells him, "the reason I could see Death."

Charlie doesn't know what Kimmy is talking about. None of it makes sense.

Kim runs upstairs and he follows. She grabs a scythe. Black robes swirl and envelop her body, and Charlie's eyes go wide. This creature is not his sweet daughter. This vile thing is an impostor coming to take him away from his family! The cowled figure grabs him, tugs his arm, and places him in its pocket. It's pitch dark in there, and terror grips him. He's never been so lost and confused. He prays this is all a bad dream.

When Charlie emerges from the Grim Reaper's black pocket, he stands on a bridge. The place looks familiar, and it gives him a terrible feeling, perhaps worse than the darkness of the Reaper's pocket. Charlie can tell it's also taking all the Reaper's power to be on this bridge. Even though he cannot see Death's expression, he can tell she's distraught. She doesn't want to be here, and neither does he.

A hazy and incomplete memory pokes at the back of Charlie's mind. Becca is driving. They are arguing. Something bounds into their lane—*a herd of spooked deer? No, it was four jet-black horses, near impossible to see in the dark. Where had they come from?* Becca wrenches the wheel to avoid hitting the animals, and the car skids along the wet road, slamming into a guardrail. The impact is so hard that the railing tears away, and their vehicle tips over the bridge, plummeting into frigid waters. They never surface.

It's as if the Reaper sees the memory, too. Death leans her scythe against the bridge, and there is Kimmy again. Charlie falls to his knees and grabs hold of his crying daughter. "It's no one's fault," he tells her. "Sometimes things just happen, sweetheart."

He holds his daughter tighter, gripping her close, desperate to comfort her, to be there for her always, but he sees it now—he is translucent.

"Sometimes there is no big plan, Kimmy. No special reason or meaning for why things happen. But I don't feel any pain. That's good, right? But I'm so—I don't know where your mother is. Have you seen her, Kimmy? Where's Jake? We need to find them."

# Twenty-Six

Kim is somewhere she never wanted to visit again, standing on the bridge that took her parents. But at least her father is with her—his ghost, anyway. But he looks so sad and confused. He didn't know he was dead. Kim had to bring him here and show him, make him remember, even though it was the last thing she wanted to do.

*Has Mom gone ahead without Dad? He says he can't find her, but he can still feel her sometimes, which means she's close but beyond sight, somehow. Does nobody see anyone once they're dead? Are we all alone for eternity?*

Kim isn't sure how any of this works. It might always be a mystery, and maybe that's okay. She's learning to accept the unanswerable questions. The one thing she knows for sure is that her father was the reason she could see the Grim Reaper. Now, she must take him to Charon with the hope of reuniting her parents. Her dad says sometimes things happen for no reason, but sometimes they happen for the perfect reason. It can be hard to tell the difference.

Kim peers over the edge at the black river far below with its swirling eddies frozen in time. Her eye catches something up ahead, suspended in mid-air. She grasps her father's hand, and they step closer for a better view of the floating object.

*It's a person.* They must have leaped from the bridge at the exact moment Kim turned the hourglass sideways.

Kim takes another step and halts as icicles of realization crystalize in her bloodstream. Fear grips her as Kim's heart thunders in her chest.

*No, no, no!* She screams his name. "JAKE!"

# Twenty-Seven

Kim tugs at her brother's suspended body, trying to bring him up and over the side of the bridge. Their father looks on, growing agitated at his inability to help. Jake is frozen in mid-air, trapped in time, stuck in the momentum and inevitability of his choice to jump.

Kim's heart races in her chest, ready to explode in a mix of terror, anger, and grief. Seeing her brother hovering above a hundred-foot drop into freezing water is like watching a loved one die in slow motion, and you can't do anything about it. *Can* she do anything about it?

"You need to find rope—a lot of it," Charlie says. "Tie it around his waist and ankles and anchor it to the bridge, so when he keeps falling, he won't fall the whole way. Or maybe find a bungee cord. Then find a way to pull him up."

The Reaper agrees to this plan. She's grateful her father is here.

Kim shakes off her anguish and races home, back to the garage, where she knows there is a bin of heavy-duty elastic cords from all the family camping trips they used to take. She hopes they're strong enough.

Back at the bridge, Kim floats over to Jake and wraps him up in so many elastic cords that he looks like an unraveling mummy. She hooks the cords to at least six railings that line the bridge. Then, she takes the hourglass and turns it upright.

Jake falls another few feet and the cords unhook from the sudden strain, snapping free. Kim spins the hourglass sideways, halting the moment once again.

"I can't, I can't." She squeezes her eyes shut, gripped by terror, and her inability to change the choice her brother has put into motion. "He's going to break through and fall anyway. It's not strong enough."

Charlie points to his son. "Kimmy, go down there and resecure everything. Do it stronger this time. Anchor the cords around his waist and ankles. Don't worry about his arms. You can do this."

Kim does as her father instructs, floating down to secure the elastic cords again. Instead of retying the ones that broke away from the railings, she latches them to Snowball's saddle. "Dig in your hooves, girl."

Once she's re-secured everything, Kim reaches for the hourglass and tilts it upright.

Snowball slides forward a few inches, and a few cords snap free, leaving Jake suspended about fifteen feet over the side.

"What the—?" Jake gasps in alarm. "Hey! *HEYYY!*"

Kim pulls at Snowball's reins, walking the horse backward. Jake rises toward the ledge. When he's close enough to grab hold of, Kim races to him and pulls him over the side.

Jake gasps, his face pale and his breath coming in short, stuttering bursts. He begins crying, and his body caves in on itself as he covers his face in his hands. Kim holds her brother, cradling him in her arms while he sobs. Kim is crying, too. She sees what she's never seen before: how much Jake has been bottling up his feelings, trying to be the strong one for her, for everyone. He laughs everything off. They all think Jake is so fun to be around—"Never better!" as he always says—but he's in so much pain. Kim can't believe she's missed the cues, but how could she know?

How can anyone know how much another suffers? Even when they tell us, all we have is our experience and the skin we live in to go by. We try to empathize, but does anyone know or understand all that our wounded hearts hold?

"You're okay," Kim whispers into her brother's ear. "Let it out. You're okay."

When Jake stops crying, he sits up with a start. "Kimmy, what are you doing here? And whose horse is that?"

Kim doesn't know how to explain any of this to Jake. The one thing that matters to her is keeping him from trying this again. "I need you to talk to me, Jake. You can't hurt yourself. If you try this again, and it works, you won't be with Mom or Dad. Don't ask me how I know that. I just do, and I need you here. Not to take care of me, but as my brother. You're my family, and we need each other. It's that simple."

Jake stares at her through red-rimmed eyes. "They're offering me a baseball scholarship at Wake Forest."

"Oh my God, Jake, that's amazing! Why would you be so—"

"Because I can't do it, Kim. I can't ever leave here. My life is over. Everything I wanted and worked for, I'm getting, but it's still totally out of reach."

"Are you saying you can't go because of me?"

"No, not you. It's just...I'm stuck here, we both are. I'm trying to stay positive and be happy, so people don't feel sorry for me, but it's all an act, you know that. I can't take it anymore."

Kim didn't know that. She had no idea her brother felt this way. *Maybe we're not so different?*

Kim places her hands on her brother's cheeks. "Jake, look at me. Go to Wake Forest. Live your life. You're going to do great things there, and I'm going to be fine here."

"You're not. You're stuck being a little kid, and Kimmy, I don't know how to tell you this, but I don't think Grandma has much more time."

Kim stands up and squares her shoulders, looking down at her brother. "Jake Morse, I am going to be fine, so don't you dare not go to college, or worse, *kill yourself* because you can't hack your life around this stupid town. I'm fifteen. Sure, I've got some growing up to do, but if you haven't noticed, I'm no little girl. I just saved your frickin' life! And news flash: I know Grandma is dying. I've known it longer than you. All I want is for her to go in peace—to not suffer. She deserves that, right?"

Jake stares at his sister as though seeing something within her he's never seen before. *Courage. Strength. Certainty.* She still has that warmth and silliness—the striped pink and blue hair is a dead giveaway—but it's as if she's grown up five years over the past five days.

"You still haven't explained the horse."

Kim opens her mouth to speak, but the words dry up as she hears the thunderous clomping of galloping hooves.

"Uh, s-sweetheart?" Charlie whispers, the words hitching in his throat as Kim turns on her heel toward the darkness of the two-lane road—toward the three horsemen emerging from the fog at the far end of the bridge. She grabs the scythe, readying for a showdown, but she knows she's outnumbered. She dives, reaching for the upturned hourglass, but it pings off her outstretched skeletal fingers, slipping along the wet pavement, and failing to fall on its side as it slides out of reach. *No other choice now but to fight.*

Death rises with her scythe gripped in both hands. She steps forward, placing herself between the hourglass and the charging horsemen.

The Grim Reaper's sudden defensive stance confuses Jake. "Kimmy? What's—"

"Stand back, Jake. I gotta show these three dirtbags who's boss."

Wispy green smoke and acidic spittle trail from the poisoned arrowhead as it flies through the night air in an arcing motion from Martin's bow, lodging into Jake's chest. Jake doesn't see the arrow, but he staggers, goes pale, and vomits over the bridge railing. His reaction isn't because of the pain of the arrow, but from the sudden onset of debilitating flu-like symptoms. He falls to his knees, weak, feverish, and near death.

"NO!" Kim screams. She didn't save Jake from the bridge to have him die at the hands of the Horseman of Pestilence. She wants to charge at Martin and take off his head with her scythe, but she knows she cannot step too far from the hourglass, or one of the others will get to it, and then *everyone* dies.

Kim leaps backward as the horses thunder toward her. She can freeze them in place if she can get to the hourglass. She wishes she had decapitated them the last time she froze them, but she has a terrible hunch that others would take their places and start the whole battle over again. How can she get them to back off?

Luki's sword arcs towards Kim's cowled hood, and she blocks it with her scythe with a metallic *clang*! Her reactions are faster than usual—perhaps something to do with how she perceives time as the Reaper, or maybe it's the flood of adrenaline racing through her veins. Either way, she's smart enough to know she's no match for the battle-trained Horseman of War. She needs to get away from him and get to the hourglass before—

Kim's eyes widen as Peggy lifts the hourglass in triumph, readying to throw it down and shatter it. Time slows, the next second passing like a painful eternity.

Her father's ghost kneels over his son. Jake gasps on the ground with the arrow protruding from his chest. Luki readies another swing. Martin aims an arrow at the Reaper. Peggy raises the hourglass over her head, and Gwyn—*wait, what the heck is Gwyn doing here?*

The fate goddess skids in, her legs outstretched as her five-inch heeled boots connect with Peggy's wooden leg, sending the woman flying into the air and the hourglass with her. Kim doesn't even care that kicking out an amputee's wooden leg is a particularly low blow. She'll talk to Gwyn about it later. Right now, she's grateful her best friend is here.

Kim dodges away from Luki's sword thrust as the blade slices through her robes. She's too freaked out to notice if the wound has drawn blood or not. If she's a skeleton under these robes, maybe not? Either way, all she cares about is getting to that plummeting hourglass before it shatters on the ground.

Death dives, reaching out to catch the hourglass. It falls, bouncing once off her bell sleeves and coming to rest in her skeletal fingers.

Kim leaps to her feet and staggers away from the oncoming Luki. In a last-ditch effort to save the hourglass—and herself—she jumps over the side of the bridge. It's the exact thing Kim wanted Jake to promise never to do, and now she's doing it. The silver lining is that Death can float, but she's unsure how to stop herself from ending up in the icy river. *This can't be the end.* She can't sink to the bottom of the same river that took her parents. That can't be her fate!

Squeezing her eyes shut, Kim thinks of her mom and dad, and for some strange reason, this makes her think of their favorite song. She's still wearing her headphones around her neck.

The Reaper tucks the hourglass in her robes and puts on her headphones as she descends like a feather toward the black waters below. She presses play, and Cher's *If I Could Turn Back Time* begins to play. Death has a burst of inspiration bigger than any *a-ha!* moment she's ever had. This song is like a message from her mother or a clue from the universe. There's a deeper meaning here, like a secret her mother has been trying to send her from beyond.

Death retrieves the hourglass and turns it sideways. The world grinds to a halt, and she hovers in midair. Only then does she notice the poisonous green arrow mere inches from her chest.

Martin's smug look of satisfaction peers over the ledge at her. Death grins back and continues turning the hourglass until it is upside down.

The world feels as if it's about to break as its gears grind and shift in reverse. The arrow sizzles back to Martin's bow. Death rises to the bridge, lies on the ground, and tosses the hourglass into the air, back into Peggy's hands as Gwyn slides away, and Luki swings his sword away from Death. The arrow dislodges from Jake's chest and retreats into its quiver.

The reverse world speeds up, and now Kim is un-baking cupcakes. She is in Gwyn's room with her dogs.

She takes the marching band back inside the crashed bus. Everything that's happened these past few days undoes itself. The upside-down hourglass is back in Death's robes, and try as she might, she doesn't have the strength to retrieve it. Kim panics, gripping at the robes, hoping to turn the world right-side up again.

Moments later, the Reaper travels in reverse on her mighty steed, her hands busy as she takes souls from her robes and deposits them where she found them. Atomic Pink and Blue Ruin bleeds from her hair, she un-meets Gwyn at school, and she vanishes from her first meeting with Charon, the robes unraveling from her body.

The Grim Reaper, looming over Grandma's bed, sees Kim launching away from them with her baton raised high. The Reaper realizes they're moving in reverse and fumbles for the hourglass in their robes. It takes all their strength to retrieve it, and when they do, they flip it upright as Kim throws open the door to Grandma's room.

Kim stares into Death's hooded cowl and sees an eternal blackness there—a void staring back—as Death regards Kim in return. The silence is so profound it's a wonder the hourglass isn't turned on its side. Kim swallows hard as she sets the baton down, leaning it against the doorframe. She raises both hands in surrender.

"Look... I know you need to take her and I'm not gonna fight you on that. I think I understand now. But there are some things you need to know."

Death moves around the bed and approaches Kim. She's never been so terrified. *Will Death take me now? Do they know what I did?*

"So, um, first off," Kim continues, hoping for the best. "There's gonna be a girl on a highway at night. You need to take her for frozen yogurt. Also, there's a man who needs a few minutes to say goodbye to his kids. Please let him do that. And when you find the marching band at the bottom of the ravine, the only way to get them in formation is to spin your scythe like it's a majorette baton." Kim hesitantly lifts and spins her baton once as a demonstration then sets it down again. "So yeah, like that. Also, uh...my father's ghost is around here someplace. He's the reason I can see you. I mean, I don't want you to take him, but...he needs to be with my mom."

Death takes another step forward. Kim flinches, squeezing her eyes shut. When she peeks again, Death has pulled back their cowl.

Kim gasps a shuddering breath, overcome with emotion. "*Mom?*"

# Twenty-Eight

"**S**weetheart. How is your father?"

"He's really confused. I mean, I am too."

"I was afraid so." Rebecca Morse sits on the edge of the bed. Grandma stirs but does not awaken. "Kim, I've been a bit selfish. I wasn't ready to let your father go to the other side without me. And I knew you and Jake weren't ready to assume this role, which means I've had to continue as the Reaper and let your dad stay here until I was ready to go, too. I know it isn't fair to him."

"But you're here for Grandma." Kim points at the snoring woman. "Mom, if you can take your mom, why can't you take Dad?"

"You're right. Of course you are." Rebecca looks at Kim as if seeing her daughter for the first time in years. "My, how you're growing up."

"Mom, are you Death, like, I mean, for real?"

A sheepish smile creases Rebecca's lips. "It's true. We are descended from a long familial line of reapers."

"Wait. But Dad's last name is Morse. I thought his father might be Death or even him."

"Your father? Seriously? News flash: your father took my name when we married."

"He took *your* name?"

"Kimmy, don't be such a Pollyanna. Or would you rather your last name was Kimberly Juszczakiewicz?"

"Jooshta-what?"

"Right? I know. The Poles have such interesting ideas about spelling."

"I'm Polish?"

"Well, a quarter Polish at least. You're also Spanish, Scottish, Malaysian, Venezuelan, Dutch, Russian Jew and who knows what else—a real mestizo, my girl. Oh, there's so much you don't know about your family origins, and I'm sorry I never told you more while there was time."

"How long have you been doing this? I was Death for, like, four or five days, and I nearly had a nervous breakdown."

"Oh sweetheart, it's not your time yet, and you've had no training."

"But *how* do you do it? How did you keep up and collect all those souls every day with a career and raising kids on top of it?"

"Well, I was exhausted most days, but I'd have been exhausted even without this part of my life. In truth, stopping time whenever I needed a nice, long nap came in quite handy."

"But how did you collect so many souls? I had to stuff them in my pockets and lead them with my scythe like it was a majorette baton. It took me months to do one night's work."

Rebecca laughs. "Oh, Kim. In your pockets? That's not—I mean, are you saying you went looking for souls?"

"Of course. How else do you find them?"

Rebecca places an open palm on her daughter's heart. Kim has a vision of Death gliding through the world, taking in all its beauty. Death gazes upon every grain of falling sand and puts its essence into her heart, creating an invisible thread that binds it to her. She does not travel to find them—she calls them to her side, like an empathetic magnet. Once there, they walk with Death, and Death walks with them, *Home*.

The Reaper takes her hand away from her daughter's chest. "As Ram Dass once said, 'We are all just walking each other home.' You understand, my sweet girl?"

A flood of emotion overwhelms Kim. "I do, Mom."

"Practice this in your daily life. Remember it all your waking days, and when the time comes, and I am ready to discover what lies beyond that great sunrise, you will have another chance to take-up the scythe. You can always say no. Perhaps one day you or Jake will have a child who will assume the role? But we are Morses, my dear one. This is what we do, and the part we play in this great celestial dramedy of life and love. I don't have the answers, but I commit to be of service, regardless. What I do know is that this is the only place in our vast three-dimensional universe where it's possible to experience both life and love. There is so much more beyond this world. Trust in that, and revel in your short time here. Can you do that?"

"I'll try, but...I miss you and Daddy so much."

"Oh, Kimmy, I'm always close. I can smell those cookies and cupcakes whenever you bake them, and the love I hold for you, deep within my soul, whisks me to your side. Every time."

Kim wipes away tears. "I feel you with me whenever I bake."

"Yes, because I'm there. You can call on Dad, Grandma—and even Charon—or anyone else who's moved beyond this mortal world. The veil that separates us is as thin as a sheet of paper, my love." Mom smiles. "We are that close anytime you need us."

# Twenty-Nine

The next few days are hard for Kim. The trouble starts when she wakes up her brother to tell him Grandma has died. After that comes funeral arrangements and a eulogy written by Kim, followed by a challenging conversation with Jake about his mental state. Kim knows what he plans to do a few days from now. She can't tell him outright that she can see the near future, but still, she can let him know how much she loves him and how important it is that he take every opportunity that comes his way—also how important it is that he process his emotions in a healthy way before they weigh him down and bury him. She suggests they may need some family counseling at long last. Jake agrees.

"How did my kid sister get so smart?"

Kim narrows her eyes. "I've always been smart! It's just that I'm no longer afraid to speak up or do scary things."

"I can tell. There's still a lot we need to figure out, but at least you're handling all this way better than me," Jake admits.

"I'm doing my best. That's all either of us can do."

Kim and Jake miss the majority of their first week of high school—but it's not the end of the world. *Not by a long shot.* Kim's confident they'll both catch up with some extra effort.

On the day they return to school, Kim is ready and waiting when her brother comes downstairs. "We got this," she tells him.

Jake agrees and hugs his sister—a genuine heart-against-heart embrace—the first one he's given her in years.

It isn't until Kim reaches the Sunderland High parking lot that she has a sudden sense of dread. She's not Death anymore. Gwyn won't be here. She wouldn't have transferred schools. *Does it mean we never meet?*

Kim walks the halls, forlorn and mopey, but when she sees Taylor Mead, she smiles. "Hey," Kim says, not caring what Taylor thinks of her, or if she's lead majorette, or even if she decides to call her a baby. *So what?*

Taylor narrows her eyes, suspicious that Kim is daring to speak to her. "Hey?"

Kim leans against the locker next to Taylor. "So here's the thing, Tay-Tay: I know we used to be close, and I'm not sure what happened between us. I was going through a lot, as you know, and I'm sure it might have felt like I let it overshadow our friendship, but sometimes friends drift apart, and that's cool. I just wanted to say I wish you all the best and harbor no hard feelings. I hope you feel the same."

"Um, yeah, cool." Taylor seems unaccustomed to anyone confronting her with straight talk.

"Great." Kim turns to go.

"It's just that," Taylor begins, her voice quiet. Kim turns to face her. "Yeah, you missed my birthday. We had promised to have our first kisses that day—you with Finley Mavet, and me with Dylan Baldwin—but you never showed, and I know you had your reasons, but because you never kissed Fin, I never kissed Dylan and then a week later he was going with Addison and then that summer he moved away, and I kinda blamed you for flaking out on the kiss...and for ruining my future." Taylor shakes her head. "Oh my God, it's so stupid when I say it out loud."

Kim nods slowly. "Yeah, it kinda is. But I get it."

Taylor looks Kim up and down, from her black boots to her gray sweater. "You seem super-different this year."

"We're in high school. Gotta grow up some time, I guess. But there's no way I'm giving up this badass star unicorn backpack."

Taylor laughs. "I can see that."

"Anyway," Kim turns to go. "I'll see you in class."

"See ya 'round, Kim Morse."

# Thirty

Kim stands in the quad after school. A sea of kids stroll by in all directions, laughing, jostling, joking, and smelling not-so-awesome. As they all depart for home, Kim stands alone, not yet ready to walk to the parking lot and catch a ride home with Jake. She's thinking about heading to the pharmacy and buying hair dye.

Then Kim sees her across the green lawn, leaning against a tree.

She runs into Gwyn's waiting embrace. "You remembered me."

"Don't be silly, my annwyn. How could anyone forget you?"

Kim pulls away and looks Gwyn in the eye with a devilish grin. "So, I have this really amazing idea."

"Does it involve coloring our hair and going to the Home Day's parade together?"

Kim laughs. "That *is* an amazing idea, but I have one even better."

# Thirty-One

The scent of fresh-baked sea-salt chocolate-chip cookies permeates the house. Kim paces her room, talking on the phone. Though one wall has a fresh coat of blue and pink stripes, the other three are now white. A large painting of a sunset by J.M.W. Turner is on the wall above her bed. Kim picked out the picture because it reminded her of a place she once visited, when she met a kind-hearted ferryman.

Kim crosses the hall as she finishes her call and steps into Jake's old bedroom. Gwyn looks up and smiles. "Was that your brother?"

Gwyn sits on her black blanketed bed. All her things are here in Jake's old room—from her Bauhaus posters to her wolf skull.

Kim tucks her phone into the back pocket of her black jeans. "Yeah. He's just checking in, you know how he gets."

"I do. How's he liking college?"

Kim flops onto the bed next to Gwyn. "He seems to be loving it. Weird that he's so far away, though. Even weirder that he calls your mom at least twice a week to check on me."

"Well, it's super-cool that he's letting my mom and me live here rent-free in exchange for looking after you until you finish high school."

Kim nudges Gwyn. "You make it sound like you're babysitting."

"Of course not! It's the most brilliant idea ever and I'm shocked you thought of it."

"Oh, is that so? I'll have you know I'm the queen of creative ideas."

Gwyn huffs. "Uh-huh. Speaking of creative, how's that class you're taking at the community college with the infamous Mrs. Bell? I can't believe you actually signed up to see her outside of school."

Kim brightens. "Oh, I love her class so much."

"So, what are you working on?"

"Um, I'm kinda writing a fantasy story that's also a little bit horror genre with some supernatural elements and maybe sorta coming-of-age?"

"Eh, sounds cool. I think. You're doing your author-speak again. I meant, what's it about?"

"It's about a teenage girl who has to cover for the Grim Reaper for the week."

"Isn't that just a memoir? Or a black comedy? Anyway, I like it. Got a title yet?"

"I'm calling it Gwyn Reaper."

Gwyn bolts upright from the bed, eyes sparkling and grinning ear-to-ear. "You cutie."

Kim smiles. "Love ya, babe."

Gwyn leans close and whispers, "Caru ti hefyd."

Kim scrunches her nose. "What's that mean?"

Gwyn's eyes flutter closed as she brushes her lips against Kim's lips. Kim surrenders to Gwyn's soft mouth, a flood of butterflies erupting in her stomach and a heat swelling in her chest. Their kiss is sweet and perfect, and for the first time in Kim's life, time truly stops.

Kim stirs from a deep sleep and awakens to a bright blue sky. She stretches. There's nothing better than sleeping in on a summer morning. There is also nothing worse than an incessant knocking coming from the front door at 6:15 a.m.

"Ughhh, somebody get that." The banging continues as Kim rolls out of bed and staggers downstairs to see who the heck is ruining her first day of summer vacation.

Kim frowns when she opens the door. "Um. Fin? Are you okay?"

Finley Mavet takes up the entire doorframe, but he's like a timid mouse. He's sweating like he ran the whole way.

"I had to come here right away and talk to you."

Kim feels cold all over. *Dear Lord, don't let him ask me to be his girlfriend this summer.* "Um, sure. What?"

"I had this crazy dream that this super-old guy came to me, like, with a white beard and stuff."

"Like Santa?"

"No, it was longer. He said he was my great-great-great, honestly, I don't know how many greats he said, at least eight, or maybe it was nine?" Finley's voice trails off.

"And? Your great what?"

"Sorry, my great-grandfather. And he told me to tell you that your mom is in trouble and needs your help."

"My mom?"

"I know. I know she died like six years ago, and I tried to tell the old guy that, and then his voice got all booming, and he told me not to be a nincompoop and to let you know right away."

Kim goes cold. She thinks she may know this old man. "Did he say where my mom was?"

"No, but he said I had to help you find her and to tell Gwyn too."

"Tell me what?" Gwyn steps up behind Kim wearing an oversized Babes in Toyland concert tee as a dress. Kim marvels that Gwyn has already reapplied her black eye makeup before coming downstairs.

"Um, you look nice."

"Thanks, babe. What's the morning tea Fin's serving?"

"Yeah, so, Fin was telling me he had a dream that an old guy came to see him and said my mom was in trouble and needed our help."

"Your mom? What old guy?"

Kim leans into Gwyn's neck and whispers, "I think it might be Charon."

Fin points. "That's the name he said!"

Kim's eyes go wide. "Charon is your great-great-great—"

"Focus, Kim." Gwyn interrupts, her expression turning urgent as she steps closer to Fin, who instinctively steps away from the scary goth girl. "Did he mention anything about a scythe?"

Fin seems confused. "Last thing he said was that we all needed to sign-up for some summer camp to find Kim's mom."

"What?" Kim thinks this dream Fin had might be one of Charon's practical jokes. *Did Charon pull pranks?*

"Did he say the name of the camp?" Gwyn asks, her gaze intent on Fin.

"Camp Fire Lake."

Gwyn bites her lower lip, her face contorting, about to explode. "The lake of fire. *The second death*."

Kim and Fin wait for Gwyn to say more. None of it makes sense to them.

Gwyn places her hands on Kim's shoulders. "Babe, the horsemen have your mom."

Kim's face pales. "What? So, who has the hourglass?"

# Discussion Questions

1. What are the main themes or messages of the book?

2. What are some of the passages that really stuck with you, and why?

3. Did the book change your opinion about anything?

4. What does Kim learn throughout the story? What are some coping skills she picks up?

5. Which character do you most relate to, and why?

6. How do the characters' relationships impact how the story unfolds?

7. What are some ways Kim and Jake dealt with the loss of their parents differently? Are there any ways in which they were similar?

8. Jake and Taylor are both great examples of not always knowing what a person is struggling with behind what they show to the world. After finding out why they act the way they do, does it change your opinion of them?

9. Were the story's depictions of death, grief, and loss different from what you expected?

10. If you could ask Charon the ferryman one question about life, what would it be?

# Acknowledgements

Thank you to my wife, Renee, and my daughter, Simone, for taking turns reading my first draft aloud so I could hear what a mess it was and make it better.

In crafting Kim's character, I borrowed elements from my childhood, stories I've heard from my wife's childhood, and the things I've witnessed watching my daughter grow up. In a very real sense, Kim is a celebration of my family, and I will always adore her for that. She also helped me get over the loss of my father, so this one is for him.

Thanks to my wonderful writer friends, Craig E. Sawyer and Francesca Maria, for beta-reading this book and giving me such encouraging and insightful feedback. Writing (like many creative endeavors) tends to be a solitary experience, and I am so grateful for my writing community. And, of course, huge thanks to everyone at Graveside Press—Kelley, Hannah, and Steven—for giving this story the perfect home.

Gregg Stewart is an author, HWA-member, award-winning songwriter, musician, screenwriter, journalist, film composer, and public speaker, whose dark fiction tales have appeared in multiple print anthologies including *Hotel Macabre Vol 1, Shallow Waters, Dead Letters: Tales of Epistolary Horror* (Crystal Lake), *To Hell and Back* (HellboundUK), *Black Cat Tales*, and *Best of Sleyhouse 2025*. He has recorded and published over 100 songs, toured the US and Europe countless times, placed songs in a dozen movies and tv series, and provided the score for multiple indie films. His nonfiction book, *LET IT OUT: Unlocking Creativity to Access Authentic Expression* reached #7 on Amazon's best sellers for new releases in creativity.

BlueSky @greggstewart
Twitter/X @thegreggstewart
Instagram @thatgreggstewart

# content warnings

**Intended for readers 12+**


bullying

death of parents and loved ones

death of children (off-page/implied)

fatphobic comments (addressed on-page)

mental health struggles

attempted suicide (jumping from a bridge)

# Thank You!

Thank you for supporting Graveside Press and our authors. One of the biggest ways you can help is to leave a star rating or a review wherever you purchased your copy!

## Stay spooky.

graveside-press.com

Want to get discounts on future Graveside books?
gsp-shop.fourthwall.com